Aubrey Stewart

The Tale of Troy

Aubrey Stewart

The Tale of Troy

ISBN/EAN: 9783337072674

Printed in Europe, USA, Canada, Australia, Japan

Cover: Foto ©Andreas Hilbeck / pixelio.de

More available books at **www.hansebooks.com**

THE

TALE OF TROY

DONE INTO ENGLISH

BY

AUBREY STEWART, M.A.

LATE FELLOW OF TRINITY COLLEGE,
CAMBRIDGE.

London

MACMILLAN AND CO.

AND NEW YORK

1886

CONTENTS

CHAP.   PAGE

I.   *How Paris carried off Helen*   .   I

II. *How the Heroes gathered at Aulis*   13

III. *How   Achilles   quarrelled   with
     Agamemnon* 27

IV. *How Paris fought Menelaus*   . 45

V.   *How Hector fought Ajax*   .   . 61

VI. *How Hector tried to burn the Ships* 87

VII. *How Patroclus lost the Arms of
     Achilles*   109

VIII. *How Achilles slew Hector*   .   . 129

IX. *How the Greeks fought the Amazons* 147

X.   *How Paris slew Achilles*   .   . 167

XI. *How Philoctetes slew Paris*   . 193

XII. *How the Greeks took Troy* .   . 215

HOW PARIS CARRIED OFF HELEN

B

CHAPTER I

How Paris carried off Helen

ONCE upon a time there lived a king and queen, named Tyndareus and Leda. Their home was Sparta, in the pleasant vale of Laconia, beside the river Eurotas. They had four children, and these were so beautiful that men doubted whether they were indeed born of mortal parents. Their two sons were named Castor and Polydeuces. As they grew up, Castor became a famous horseman, and Polydeuces was the best boxer of his time. Their elder daughter, Clytemnestra, was wedded to Agamemnon the son of Atreus, king of Mycenae, who was the greatest prince of his age throughout all the land of Hellas. Her sister Helen was the loveliest woman ever seen upon earth, and every prince in Hellas wooed her for his bride; yet was her beauty fated to bring sorrow and destruction upon all who looked upon her. The suitors of Helen were many, and were so fierce in their wooing that their threats affrighted Tyndareus, who was old and feeble; for each one vowed that if he did not win her hand he would wreak a fearful vengeance both on the rival who should be preferred to him and on the family of the bride. At last Tyndareus made all the suitors agree to swear a mighty oath, that, whosoever among them might become the husband of Helen, they would all stand by him, and help him to win back his wife if any one robbed him of her. After this, Tyndareus bade Helen herself choose out of all her suitors the one whom she loved best for her husband. She chose Menelaus, the brother of Agamemnon; and when they were wedded, Tyndareus gave up his kingdom to his son-in-law, and Menelaus and his wife reigned in Sparta.

Far away, across the blue Ægean, was the city of Troy, standing on a hill in the plain between Mount Ida and the sea, on the southern shore of the Hellespont, the strait over which Phrixus and his sister Helle swam on the back of the ram with the golden fleece. But Helle slipped off into the sea and was drowned, and so the strait is called the Hellespont to this day. The king of Troy was rich and mighty; he dwelt in a stately palace, built of polished stone, and stored with corn and wine; his flocks were pastured on Mount Ida, and his city was the greatest on all the Asian coast. His name was Priam, and his eldest son was named Hector. Just before his second son Paris was born, his queen, Hecuba, dreamed that she had brought into the world a flaming torch, by which all the city of Troy was set in a blaze. So, when Paris was born, they felt sure that he would bring misfortune upon them; yet they had not the heart to kill the babe, but took it away out of the city, and left it in a thicket on Mount Ida. Here a shepherd found it and brought it up as his own child. Some say that it was he who gave the boy the name of Paris; but when he grew up, the other shepherds called him Alexander, which means "Defender of men," because he fought bravely, as a king's son should, and defended them and their flocks from wild beasts and savage men. He grew up to be a tall and goodly youth, and dwelt as a shepherd on Mount Ida, loving and beloved by the nymph Œnone, the daughter of Kebren, the river-god, never dreaming that he was a prince, and the son of King Priam of Troy.

Meanwhile at Phthia in Thessaly there came about the famous wedding of Peleus, king of the Myrmidons, with Thetis, the silver-footed goddess of the sea, whom he caught in a cave by the seashore, and held fast, though she tried to slip from his grasp by enchantment, and changed her shape seven times. She changed to water, to vapour, and to burning flame; and to a rock, and to a black-maned lion, and to a tall and stately tree. But Peleus remembered what Cheiron, the wise old Centaur, had taught him, and held her fast until she returned to her own shape again, and promised to be his bride. All the gods of Olympus came to their wedding, rejoicing at the marriage of an Immortal with a mortal man. Thither came Zeus, the father of gods and men, and Hêrê his wife, and Pallas Athênê the wise, and beauteous Aphrodite. Thither, too, came the Parcae, the Fates that spin the thread of every man's life, bearing their distaffs in their left hands, forming the thread and twirling the spindle with their right, while with their withered lips they chanted a prophecy about the child that should be born of that marriage.

Now Eris, the goddess of strife, had not been bidden to the wedding with the rest of the Immortals. In her anger she came and threw among the guests, as they sate at table in the hall of Peleus, a golden apple, on which was written " For the fairest." It was straightway claimed by each of the three goddesses, Hêrê, Athênê, and Aphrodite ; and then arose quarrelling and discord, because no one could prove for which goddess it was meant. At last Father Zeus, to put an end to the strife, bade Iris, the swift messenger of the gods, take the apple to Paris, the shepherd of Mount Ida, and bid him give it to her whom he might deem the fairest of the three.

It was a still midsummer noon on Mount Ida : the cicalas chirped shrilly in the bushes, and the gray lizards were basking on the warm rocks, but all other creatures had sought shelter from the heat, and Paris's flock lay in the cool shade beside a fountain when the three goddesses appeared on the wide lawn before him. The radiance of their beauty filled all the air, and bright-hued flowers sprang up from the turf whereon they trod, as they stood revealed to his gaze. First of the three spake Hêrê, the queen of Olympus.

"Give me the apple, Paris. You are already a king's son, although you know it not ; and I will make you the richest and mightiest king in all the world. You shall reign over stately cities, and shall be the lord of wide lands, cornfield and pasture, guarded by strong castles on the hill-tops, with fair havens by the seashore, thronged with count-less masts. All neighbour kings shall do you homage, and you shall dwell all your life in happy, peaceful power like a god."

Paris, as he listened, was half-inclined to give the apple to Hêrê; but he waited till Pallas Athênê spoke. She said :

" I will teach you to become the wisest, the noblest, and the most famous of mankind. You shall know your own heart, and you shall guide the hearts of men into the ways of truth and holiness. You shall do right and fear not, and shall teach men to live happy under just and equal laws. So shall you be great and good, loved and reverenced by all."

Then Paris felt that it would be best for him to give the apple to Pallas : Œnone, who had hidden herself in a thick copse behind him, tried to whisper to him, " Give it to Pallas ; " but he did not hear her, or think of her, for at that moment glorious Aphrodite stood smiling before him, and said, " I will give you the loveliest woman on earth to be your bride."

Then Paris doubted no longer, but gave her the apple.

After Paris had given the apple to Aphrodite on Mount Ida, he could no longer be content to live the peaceful life of a shepherd. He went forthwith to Troy, and made himself known to his father Priam, and his mother Hecuba, who had thought that he was dead, and they bade him welcome to his home, and rejoiced over him. He soon forgot all about his poor Œnone, for the discovery of his royal birth had set his fancies roaming, and now he and his brothers began to cut down pine-trees on Mount Ida ; and Phereclus, the cunning workman, built ships for them, that they might go forth and see the world, and seek that beauteous bride for Paris whom Aphrodite had promised him. Helenus, the brother of Paris, and Cassandra, his sister, both of whom Phoebus loved, and breathed upon them the spirit of prophecy, earnestly besought him not to set sail, assuring him that the ships would prove the beginning of sorrows for all the Trojans. But Paris only laughed

at their gloomy forebodings, and sailed merrily
away over the rippling waters, past Lesbos,
and Chios, and through the Cyclades, the
sweet Summer Isles that girdle holy Delos,
until he came to the mainland of Peloponnesus,
and ran his ships upon the shore of the
Laconian coast.

When Menelaus, the king of Sparta, heard
that Paris was come, he went down to the
seashore and welcomed him, and bade him
haul up his ships on the beach, and come
with him and feast in his palace.   Paris
went gladly with Menelaus to Sparta, and
there his eyes fell upon Helen, Menelaus's
wife.   As soon as he beheld her, he knew
that it must be she and none other whom
Aphrodite had promised him for his own;
and when presently Menelaus departed on a
journey to King Idomeneus in Crete, Paris,
in his absence, treacherously made love to
Helen, and beguiled her to bring all the
treasure of Menelaus on board of the Trojan
ships, and to fly with him across the sea to
Troy.

HOW THE HEROES GATHERED
AT AULIS

CHAPTER II

How the Heroes gathered at Aulis

NOW Hêrê, the queen of Olympus, hated Paris, because he had slighted her and given the apple to Aphrodite. Forthwith she sent the swift Iris, the messenger of the Immortals, to Menelaus, bidding him hasten home from Crete, for Paris had carried off his bride. So Menelaus sailed home with all speed, and found his house robbed, and his wife gone. As he looked round his desolate home, and thought of his lost Helen, he remembered how happy he had been with her, and felt that he must win her back again or die. But when he thought how beautiful she was, he knew in his heart that Paris would never give her up

unless he was forced, and how could he force
Paris to restore her, seeing that Troy was so
far away beyond the sea, and Priam was so
mighty a king? At last Menelaus bethought
him that he would go to Mycenae, to take
counsel with his brother Agamemnon, and to
entreat his help.

When Menelaus drove his chariot up to
the gate of the palace at Mycenae he found
his brother Agamemnon, by good hap, talking
with Nestor, the silver-tongued old man, who
was king of sandy Pylos. Old as he was, Nestor
was still as full of spirit as when, many a year
before, he sailed with Jason in the ship Argo,
to bring back the golden fleece. He, too, had
seen Helen, and grieved for Menelaus ; so,
when the brothers asked him to advise them
what to do, he straightway answered that he
would go to Euboea, and seek out Palamedes,
who was deemed to be the wisest of the Greeks,
and then they two would go round to all the
princes who had been suitors of Helen, and
call upon them to remember the oath which they
had sworn, and help Menelaus to win her back.

Now Hêrê and Athênê, out of their hatred
for Paris, stirred the hearts of the princes of
Hellas; and they all agreed to come with
ships and men, and follow Agamemnon as their
leader, until either Troy was taken, or Helen
was given back. The host gathered at Aulis
on the seashore, over against the long island
of Euboea, and the heart of Agamemnon
swelled with pride as he saw the endless
ranks of men pouring forth from their ships
and their tents, like the great flocks of cranes
and wild swans that love to settle upon the
meadows by the river Cäyster, till all the
plain resounds with the clang of their wings :
or like the countless flies that swarm round
the kine in early summer, when the fresh
milk froths in the pails.

Amid the host stood the chiefs, each marshalling his own followers, even as shepherds
separate their flocks when they have been
feeding together in one pasture; while great
Agamemnon overlooked them all, like the
lordly bull as he proudly stands amid the
heifers of the herd. There was Diomedes,

son of Tydeus, the lord of Argos, with all the men of Argolis, of Epidaurus, with its clustering vines, and of the well-walled city of Tiryns. From Pylos came old Nestor, with his two brave sons, Antilochus and Thrasymedes ; and Idomeneus, with his trusty comrade Meriones, brought eighty ships from Crete.

The men of Cephallene, and Ithaca, and leafy Neritus, the isles in the far Western main, were led by Odysseus, their crafty king. Men say that he was loth to leave his newly-wedded bride Penelope, and sail over the sea to fight before Troy, and so he feigned to be mad, and ploughed the sea-sand with a yoke of oxen. But Palamedes was more cunning even than Odysseus, for he took Telemachus, the infant son of Odysseus, and laid him in the furrow before the ploughshare. Odysseus would not kill his own child, but stopped the oxen. Then Palamedes saw that his madness was feigned, and forced him to join the host at Aulis. But Odysseus never forgave Palamedes for discovering his deceit.

The Lokrians came, led by the lesser Ajax, the son of Öileus. Though he was but of a slender build, and never wore a steel corslet, yet was. he a famous archer, and could hurl the spear as well as Agamemnon himself. Many also of the brave Arcadians were there, for Agamemnon lent them ships to cross the sea, because their own land has no sea-coast ; and Agamemmon himself led a great host from fair Mycenae, and from rich Corinth, and from well-built Cleonae, and Sicyon, where once Adrastus was king. Menelaus, too, mustered all the warriors of the hollow vale of Laconia, from Sparta, and Amyclae, and Messe, where the doves coo in the tall elms, and from many a fair city besides, to help him to win back his bride. There, too, were the sturdy Boeotians, led by Peneleus, the Thessalians of Phylake and Pyrasus under their king Protesilaus, and the wise physicians, the two sons of Asclepius, Podalirius and Machaon, brought a host from the cities of Tricca, and Œchalia, and Ithome in the plains of Thessaly, beside the upper waters of fair Peneus.

The men of Athens, the darling city of
Athênê, were led by Menestheus, and with
him came the great Ajax, son of Telamon,
and his brother Teucer the archer, with
twelve ships from Salamis: while Elephenor
led troops of the warlike Abantes, who
dwell in the long island of Euboea, where
the tide ebbs and flows past Aulis in the
straits.

From Phthia in Thessaly came the Myrmidons, led by Achilles, the son of Peleus,
the bravest hero of them all. Many a strange
story is told about his birth. As soon as he
was old enough, he had been sent to Cheiron,
the good old Centaur, to be trained by him
on Mount Pelion, as his father Peleus had
been trained before him, and Heracles, and
Æneas of Troy, and Jason who sailed in the
ship Argo and brought back the golden fleece,
and many a stout hero besides. Cheiron
taught the boy to ride, and to hunt, and to
hurl the spear : he showed him how to bind
up wounds, and to lay healing herbs upon
them, and how to sing and play upon the

harp. The boy grew active and strong, and Cheiron called him "swift-footed Achilles," for he was fleeter than the mountain deer, or the wild goats that leaped from crag to crag.

His goddess mother Thetis knew well that he was fated either to live long in inglorious ease, or else to win immortal fame, and to die in the flower of his youth. Therefore she wished him not to sail to Troy with the Greeks, and sent the fair-haired boy to Lycomedes, the king of the isle of Scyros. When he came thither, King Lycomedes dressed him like one of his own daughters, so that no one could tell that he was a man. The maidens called him Pyrrha, because of his long yellow hair ; and he loved one of them, named Deidameia, so dearly that he forgot all about the war, and his dreams of glory, and would have been content to dwell for ever in the quiet isle of Scyros. But one day a strange merchant came to the palace of Lycomedes, to show his wares, and while the girls were eagerly turning over the necklaces and brooches and rich embroidered work which he brought, Achilles, for all his woman's dress, could not help taking up in his hands a fine shield and spear which the merchant had cunningly laid before him. Then Odysseus, for it was he who, disguised as a merchant, had come to seek Achilles, told him that he was found at last, and that he must leave Scyros, and lead the Myrmidons to Troy.

And, leading the men of Methone, and Meliboea, and Olizon on the crag, the towns which stand on the long rocky cape that looks towards Euboea, came Philoctetes, the trusty comrade of Heracles. Heracles now had finished all his labours, and had been taken by his father Zeus to rest on Olympus for ever; but ere he left the earth he gave his bow and arrows to Philoctetes. These arrows had been dipped in the venom of the Lernaean hydra, after Heracles had slain the monster; and while he was at Aulis, Philoctetes let one of them fall upon his foot. The poison ran through his veins straightway, and he limped and cried aloud in his agony. Yet was his courage unabated, and he hoped,

in spite of his wound, to sail with the rest
of the heroes to Troy.

And how they sailed to Troy I hardly
know; for some of the old songs say that at
first they missed their way, and landed in
Teuthrania, where Telephus, the king of that
land, attacked them, but was wounded by
Achilles. After this they sailed back to
Hellas, and Telephus was told by an oracle
to come to Hellas also, and there Achilles
healed his wounds.

But all agree that Agamemnon's boast-
fulness displeased Artemis : for his heart
swelled with pride at the sight of the great
host of which he was the chief, till he forgot
that he was mortal, and went a-hunting in the
sacred grove, within the precincts of the temple
of Artemis. Here he shot one of the favourite
deer of the goddess ; and she punished him by
sending north-easterly winds, so that the fleet
could not put to sea. Long the heroes waited
for a change of wind, but at last the prophet
Calchas told all the chiefs that until Agamemnon made atonement for his sin, they

never could leave Aulis. When Agamemnon asked what the goddess would have him do to prove his repentance, Calchas told him that a cruel sacrifice must be made; for the wrath of the goddess could not be turned away unless his own daughter, Iphigenia, were offered as a victim upon her altar.

It was hard for Agamemnon to consent to the death of his daughter, the delight of his home: and hard, too, for him to be deserted by the princes of Hellas, and forced to give up the voyage to Troy. But the patience of the chiefs was worn out by the long delay, and they insisted that the maiden should be brought to Aulis and sacrificed forthwith. Odysseus was sent to Mycenae, and by his artful wiles wrought upon Clytemnestra, the wife of Agamemnon, to bring Iphigenia to Aulis. The poor child was told that she was sent thither to be married to Achilles, and her mother gladly gave her consent to the journey, rejoicing at the thought that she was to wed the bravest of the Greeks.

Her mother Clytemnestra and her little

brother Orestes came to Aulis with Iphigenia : but when they arrived there she
learned that she had not come to be wedded,
but to be put to death.   Achilles, when
Clytemnestra told him of the deceit which
had been practised upon Iphigenia, tried to
save her, but to no purpose, since all the host
was eager for her death.   Iphigenia herself
did no discredit to her royal birth.   When the
fierce priest Calchas told her that she must
die, she looked around for help, but read her
fate in the hard looks of the kings.   When
she turned towards her father, he hid his face
in his robe and wept; and then, seeing that
her fate was sealed, she proudly walked up
to the altar alone, in maidenly beauty, begged
that no one would lay hands upon her, and
offered her throat to the knife.   But at that
moment Artemis, out of pity for her and
love for her courage, snatched her away in
a cloud, and placed her in her own temple
among the wild Sarmatians, in the Tauric
Chersonese, where she dwelt as the priestess
of Artemis for many a year.

HOW ACHILLES QUARRELLED
WITH AGAMEMNON

CHAPTER III

How Achilles quarrelled with Agamemnon

AFTER the sacrifice of Iphigenia the fleet set sail for Troy. During the voyage poor Philoctetes suffered cruelly with the wound in his foot, for the poison ran through his veins like fire, and the hurt gangrened so that his friends could not bear to have him in the ship with them. By the advice of Odysseus they landed him on the lonely isle of Lemnos, with his bow and arrows to shoot birds for food. And there he found a cave to live in, and limped about the island for many a weary day.

Meanwhile the Greeks sailed to the island of Tenedos, off the coast of the Troad, and they agreed that before disembarking on the mainland, they would send ambassadors to Troy, to ask the Trojans to give back Helen and the stolen treasure. They sent Menelaus, because it was he who had been wronged, and with him Odysseus, because he was the wisest of the Greeks, and the most cunning of speech.

When Odysseus and Menelaus came to Troy, Antenor, a noble Trojan, bade them welcome, and hospitably entertained them. Both he and King Priam wished to give back Helen and the plunder ; and on the morrow, when Menelaus and Odysseus spoke before all the people, they hoped to prevail upon Paris to give her up. But it was in vain that Menelaus begged for his wife, and that Odysseus tried to charm the Trojans with his persuasive tongue; for Paris, and his younger brothers, and all who had sailed with him to Sparta, became so enraged that they would have slain them both, if the elders had not held them back. So Odysseus and Menelaus were forced to return to the Greeks at Tenedos, and gave up all hope of winning back Helen unless they could take Troy.

Now the Trojans had not been idle, but when they heard of the great host which was coming against them, they too mustered their forces and called upon their allies to help them. There was Hector of the glancing helm, the eldest and bravest of the sons of Priam, the chief of the Trojan warriors; and his cousin Æneas, son of Anchises and the goddess Aphrodite, who led the Dardans from the ancient city of Dardania in the hills, which was built by old King Dardanus long before Troy itself was founded on the plain. Pandarus also, · the famous archer, led the men of the city of Zeleia, which stands on the roots of Mount Ida, beside the dark waters of Æsepus. From ancient Percote, and Sestos and Abydos, where Leander used to swim across the Hellespont to his love, came many brass-clad warriors, led by Asius, the son of Hyrtacus; and from every nation on the coast, from Thrace in the far north to Lycia in the south, the

country of Glaucus and Sarpedon, came King
Priam's allies, eager to fight for the fair
city of Troy. Messengers had been sent to
King Eioneus in farthest Thrace, and to
the godlike Memnon, the lord of Æthiopia,
to beg them come and help the Trojans :
but these princes dwelt far away, and it was
not yet known whether they would come
at all.

When the Greeks landed, they found all
the Trojan host drawn up to fight them.
Protesilaus was the first to run his ship on to
the beach, and to leap ashore ; but no sooner
had he touched Trojan soil than he fell,
mortally wounded by Hector's spear. Yet
in spite of this mischance, the rest of the
Greeks poured boldly on to the beach, and a
great and terrible battle began. Hector, and
Cycnus, the son of Poseidon, cut down the
Greeks as reapers cut down the thick corn ;
while Achilles, who had now landed, drove
his chariot along the line of the ships, seeking
for some worthy antagonist. Soon he caught
sight of the great Cycnus slaughtering all

around him, and straightway attacked him.
Yet, though Achilles dealt Cycnus a mighty
blow with his spear, it recoiled from his
breast, for no steel could wound him, and
Cycnus, laughing, hurled his spear against
Achilles with such force that it passed through
his brazen shield, and through nine of the
ten bulls' hides beneath the brass. A second
and a third time Achilles struck full on the
breast of Cycnus with his spear: yet no
wound followed the blow, nor was any blood
drawn from his skin. Astonished, Achilles
looked narrowly at the head of his spear,
which he thought must have come off : and
finding it still firm on the shaft, he hurled
the spear at one of the crowd, a Lycian
named Menoetes. The tough Pelian ash
passed through his breastplate, and struck
deep into his lungs. Menoetes sank to the
earth with a groan, and Achilles, as he drew
his spear from the corpse, said, " My hand
and my spear are still the same. Why, then,
can I not wound this man ? " Saying thus,
he again hurled his spear against Cycnus.

D

He took good aim, and Cycnus did not flinch from the blow, yet back rebounded the spear from his shoulder as though it had struck a wall. Where it struck, it left a trace of blood, and for a moment Achilles thought that he had at last dealt his foe a wound, but soon he saw that it was the blood of the miserable Menoetes, left there by his spear. Achilles now grew mad with rage. He flung aside his spear, drew his sword, and fell furiously upon Cycnus. With his shield in one hand and his sword in the other he rained upon Cycnus such a torrent of fearful blows that the giant became dizzy and blinded. As he stepped backwards to avoid Achilles, he stumbled over a great stone, and fell heavily to the ground. Achilles leaped upon him, tore off his helmet, and clutched him by the throat with both hands till he was choked.

Yet was Poseidon not unmindful of his son. Achilles called to Automedon to drive up his chariot and take the armour of Cycnus, but when he turned to strip the corpse, the armour alone lay on the plain. Cycnus was

gone, and Achilles saw only a wild swan
speeding seaward through the clear blue sky.
And, even at this day, the Greeks call a swan
" Cycnus."

The Trojans, when they saw Cycnus fall,
were much disheartened, and saw that the
day was lost. Achilles recovered his spear,
and hastened to the other side of the field,
where Hector and his brothers fought. Here
he came suddenly upon Troilus, the youngest
and handsomest of all the children of Priam,
driving a chariot. When Troilus found himself face to face with the terrible Achilles, his
heart died within him. With a faltering
hand he threw his spear, but it stuck harmless
in the ground. He drew his sword ; but
seeing Achilles about to hurl his mighty spear,
he dropped the sword, wheeled round his
horses, and urged them to full speed. In
vain : the spear of Achilles hurtled through
the air and pierced him through and through.
Though he fell from the car, yet his stiffening
fingers still clutched the reins, and as the
horses, mad with fright, careered along, the

spearhead through his body scored a long furrow in the sand.

The prowess of Achilles in this battle struck such fear into the Trojans, that they no longer dared to leave the shelter of their walls and fight in the open plain. As the siege seemed likely to be a long one, the Greeks, by the advice of Odysseus, dug a deep ditch, and built a rampart with five gates in it, reaching all round their camp and ships. Meanwhile Achilles took Thebe under Placos, the city of King Eëtion, who was the father of Andromache, the wife of Hector. Achilles also stormed Lyrnessus, from whence he carried off a fair maid named Briseis, and made her his bride ; and he took many other cities on the sea-coast and the isles. Agamemnon also took for his mate Chryseis, the daughter of Chryses, the priest of Apollo, who was taken prisoner at Lyrnessus. Now when her father Chryses heard of this, he was very sorry for his daughter, and came to Agamemnon with nearly all that he possessed, to ransom her from captivity.

But Agamemnon would not give her up, and spoke roughly to the old man, bidding him begone, for it would be the worse for him if he loitered about the camp, or came a second time to offer ransom for his daughter. So poor old Chryses went away with his eyes full of tears. He walked in silence along the sea-shore until he was out of sight of the Greek camp, and then he lifted up his hands to heaven, and prayed to Apollo, his lord, to avenge his wrongs and his tears on the Greeks. And Apollo hearkened unto the prayer of his servant, and sent a grievous pestilence upon the Greeks, so that they and their horses and cattle perished daily. For nine days the plague raged among them, but on the tenth day Achilles called the Greeks together, and asked them what was to be done, as they could not bear up against the war and the plague together, but must return home if none could tell them how the plague might be stayed. Then rose Calchas the prophet, and said :

" Achilles, if you will promise to protect

me, I will tell you why it is that Apollo is wroth with us, and hath sent this plague upon us. But unless you promise, I dare not speak: for I know that I shall anger one of our great men, and the wrath of a king is as a consuming fire."

Then Achilles swore that while he lived no one should lay a finger on Calchas: and Calchas said:

"Apollo is wroth with us because Agamemnon hath misused Chryses, his priest: nor will his anger pass away before Agamemnon gives back the maid Chryseis, without ransom, to her father, and offers a burnt-sacrifice of a hundred oxen to Apollo at Chrysa to wash away his sin." Thus spoke Calchas, but at his words Agamemnon rose in fury, and said:

"Prophet of evil, you speak to me nought but words of ill-omen. Much evil have you wrought me already, and now you bid me give up my fair prize, the lovely Chryseis. Well, if it must needs be so, I will give her up for my people's good: but I must have another in her stead, for it is not meet that I alone of all the Greeks should have no prize." Achilles answered him:

"Covetous man, from whence are the Greeks to get a prize for thee? All the plunder which we took in the captured cities has been equally shared among us, and we cannot ask men to give it back again. Put thou thy trust in heaven, and when we take the well-walled city of Troy, we will recompense thee three and four fold out of the plunder."

Angrily did Agamemnon reply:

"Brave Achilles, do not deceive yourself thus, or think that I will go without a prize while you keep yours. If the Greeks choose to give me some maiden as a present, to make amends for the loss of Chryseis, well and good. But if they do not, I will come and take one myself, either yours, or that of Ajax or of Odysseus, and it will be the worse for him to whom I come."

Then rose Achilles, and a fierce frown gathered on his brow as he spoke—

"Shameless and sordid soul, how can you

hope that the Greeks will follow such a one. I have no quarrel with the Trojans ; they never drove off my cattle or my horses, or spoiled my goods, for Phthia lies far away from Troy, across the main. It was for you, ungrateful that you are, and for Menelaus that I came to fight, and now you have forgotten this, and take away my prize, the maiden whom I laboured hard to win, and whom the Greeks bestowed on me. It is ever thus, when we storm some Trojan town : on me falls all the stress and toil of fight, but when we part the spoil, yours is the largest share. As for me, it will be best for me to sail home to Phthia, and to leave you here to gain what glory you can without me."

" Run away home," answered Agamemnon, " if so you wish. Far be it from me to beg you to stay for my sake. There are many here who will show me due respect : but I hate you, for you breathe nought but battle and strife. I know that you are mighty of hand, but it was the gods who made you so. Go home with your ships and your men, and

lord it over your Myrmidons in Phthia. I
care nought for your anger, and I will let
you know it. Since Phoebus Apollo takes
my Chryseis away, I will send her to her
home in my own ship, but I will come and
take away your prize, the beauteous Briseis,
that you may know that I am more powerful
than you, and that the rest may learn not to
compare themselves with me."

Thus he spoke: but the heart of Achilles
swelled with wrath, and he knew not whether
to draw his sword and slay the insulting king,
or to endure in silence and keep down his
anger. While he stood hesitating, his fingers
closed on the hilt of his great sword, and he
had drawn it half-way out of its sheath, when
Pallas Athênê, visible to him alone, came and
stood behind him. She laid her hand upon his
golden hair, and straightway Achilles turned
and knew her. Then said he, with the fierce
gleam still in his eyes :

"Goddess Athênê, wherefore art thou
here?" And Athênê answered—

"I am come to calm your anger, if you

will obey me.   Hêrê has sent me, for she
loves and fears for you both.   Wherefore
quarrel no more, and put back your sword
into its sheath.   Ere long Agamemnon shall
make ample amends to you for this insult, if
you will do as we command."

Then said Achilles, " I cannot strive against
the gods.   Be it so."   With his strong hand
he drove the sword back into its sheath ; and
Pallas Athênê vanished out of his sight, away
to Olympus the holy hill.

Wrathfully then spoke Achilles to Agamemnon.

" Insolent craven, never have you dared
to lead the host in battle, or to lie in ambush
with a chosen few, which is what tries a
man's courage, for you fear to look on death.
Far easier is it, no doubt, to plunder those
who thwart your will ; a tyrant king, because
you rule a race of cowards.   But hearken,
while I swear a mighty oath.   By this my
royal sceptre, which nevermore shall bud
and put forth leaves since it was cut and
trimmed with the axe, and I bear it in my

hand, as kings are wont to do—by this I swear, that ere long you and all the Greeks shall rue the day when you insulted the best warrior of you all. As for the maid, you gave her to me, and you may take her back. But dare to lay your hand on aught else of mine, in my tent or my black ship, and soon shall your life-blood reek upon my spear."

When Achilles ceased speaking, the assembly broke up. Agamemnon sent Chryseis home to her father, with a hundred oxen as a sacrifice to Apollo, and the plague was stayed. Achilles let Briseis go, but sorrowed deeply for her, and swore that neither he nor his Myrmidons should fight any more for Agamemnon. For a long time after Briseis was taken away from him Achilles sat alone by the sea-shore, idly gazing upon the dark blue waves. Then he remembered his goddess mother, and called aloud on her, stretching forth his hands towards the sea.

"Mother, I know full well that I am doomed to die in my youth. I had hoped to pass my little span of life without dishonour:

but now Agamemnon has insulted me, and taken away my prize." And Thetis heard him, as she sat in the hall of old Nereus her father, far beneath the waves. Quickly she rose and stood beside him, listening to the tale of his wrong. Then she comforted him, and bade him be of good cheer; for she herself would beg Father Zeus to give the victory to the Trojans, until the Greeks were humbled and made ample amends for the wrong they had done him.

About this time died Palamedes, who was called the wisest of the Greeks. Some say that he was drowned while fishing, but there is a dark and cruel tale about his death which I have not the heart to write down, but which you may read for yourself some day.

HOW PARIS FOUGHT MENELAUS

CHAPTER IV

How Paris fought Menelaus

NOW, in answer to the prayer of Thetis, Zeus sent a deceitful dream to Agamemnon, bidding him muster the Greeks and lead them forth to battle before the walls of Troy. Agamemnon, as soon as he awoke, called together the chiefs, and told them what he had dreamed. Moreover he said that, to the end that he might prove the spirit of the host, he meant to call an assembly, and to propose that they should all return home, and bade the chiefs hold the people back, if they showed any mind to set sail. The assembly met: but when Agamemnon proposed that they should all return home, the people ran so eagerly to launch the ships that it was all

Odysseus and the other chiefs could do to turn them back again to the assembly. When they were come together again, Thersites, the ugliest man of all who came to Troy, railed against Agamemnon with unseemly words.

" What more would you have ? " asked he, " Your tents are full of brass and iron, fair female slaves, and treasure. Do you covet the gold which is brought hither by the Trojans to ransom their sons, when I, or some other brave warrior, has taken them captive. Shame on you, coward women of Greece, for I will not call you men. Why do we not sail home in our ships, and leave this mighty chief here alone to gloat over his treasures, and to find out whether he needs our aid or no ? He has insulted Achilles, our bravest warrior ; and well is it for him that Achilles is mild of mood, else had that insult been his last."

Thus spoke Thersites, but straightway Odysseus stood by his side and said :

" Thou babbling fool ; be still. It ill becomes thee, the meanest of all our host, to revile Agamemnon, king of men. He has a right to ample spoils, and if I ever hear you play the fool again, I will strip you and flog you back to your ship." As he spoke, Odysseus with his sceptre struck Thersites a hard blow across his shoulders, and he, quivering with pain, sat down, and with horrible grimaces wiped away the tears which filled his eyes. While the Greeks, angry as they felt at the trick which had been played upon them, nevertheless laughed at Thersites, Odysseus in his turn made a speech to them. He reminded them of the shame it would bring upon them to prove false to the oath which they had sworn to old Tyndareus. It was hard, he owned, to stay year after year away from their homes, yet worst of all would it be to stay long away and go home empty-handed after all. "Then let us," said he, "endure yet a little longer, and swear not to leave the plains of Troy till Priam's rich city be ours."

At these words all clapped their hands, and said that Odysseus had spoken well. Agamemnon now bade the Greeks eat their breakfast, and counselled each man to sharpen his spear, and look well to his armour, as he meant to do battle with the Trojans until the going down of the sun.

While the chiefs of the Greeks were marshalling the host in battle array, Priam, with Antenor, Thymoetes, and some other elders of the city, sat on the tower near the Scaean gate, watching them. Old Priam, seeing Helen and her maidens coming towards the walls, called her to him, while the other old men murmured one to another :

" Indeed it is no shame for the Trojans and the mail-clad Greeks to fight for such a lady as this, for her beauty is like that of the Immortals on Olympus. Yet, lovely though she be, I would that she were gone back to Hellas, lest she bring ruin upon us and upon our children."

Thus they spoke under their breath, but Priam said :

" Come hither, dear child, and sit beside me. I blame you not, nor hold you to be the cause of the war. For that the Immortals alone must answer, but now tell me, who

is this great and stately warrior? He is not
so tall by a head as some of the others, but I
never beheld a goodlier man, nor yet one of
a nobler presence, for he looks as though he
were a king."

And Helen answered:

"Dear father-in-law, I feel ashamed in your
sight. Would that I had died ere I came
hither with your son, leaving my husband,
and kindred, and my darling child Hermione,
and all the beloved companions of my youth.
But the Fates decreed it otherwise, and therefore do I weep and pine away with grief.
Now as for what you ask me, this is Agamemnon, a mighty king and a brave warrior,
who once was my brother-in-law, wretch that
I am."

Then Priam said:

"Now tell me, dear child, who is that other
chief? He is not quite so tall as mighty
Agamemnon, but his shoulders are broader.
He has not yet put on his armour, but it
lies on the ground, while he moves through
the ranks, ranging his men in order, even

as a great ram walks through a flock of
ewes."

And Helen answered :

" That is Odysseus, from the rocky isle of
Ithaca, the wisest of the Greeks."

Then spoke Antenor.

" Lady," said he, "indeed you speak truly :
for Odysseus came to my house as an am-
bassador, and I know him well. He is not
handsome, but methought when he sent out
his deep-toned voice from his chest, and
poured forth his words like wintry flakes of
snow, that no mortal could compare with him
in power of speech."

Again Priam asked, " And who is that
other huge chief, whose broad shoulders
overtop all the rest ? " Helen answered :

" That is the bulwark of the Greeks, great
Ajax, son of Telamon. Close by his side
stands Idomeneus of Crete, and round him
throng the Cretan princes. I know Idomeneus well, for oft did he feast with
Menelaus in our house at Sparta, whenever
he came over to Peloponnesus from his island

home. And now I see many other nobles of
the Achaeans, whom I know well, and whose
names I could tell you, but I cannot see my
two brothers, Castor, the tamer of horses,
and Polydeuces, the boxer. Can it be that
they have stayed at home, or have they come
hither across the sea, and now shun the
throng of warriors because of the shame
which I have brought upon them?"

Thus she spoke, with tears in her eyes;
but they both were lying in their quiet graves,
beneath the green turf, in Laconia, their
native home.

When the armies met, the Trojans charged
with wild harsh cries, like flocks of cranes
when they fly south before the winter; but
the Greeks marched in silence. Foremost of
the Trojans, in splendid armour, was Paris,
with his bow slung across his shoulders, his
sword by his side, and two brass-tipped
javelins in his hands. As soon as Menelaus
caught sight of Paris, his soul was stirred
with a fierce joy, for now he deemed his
hour of vengeance was at hand. He sprang

from his car, and rushed towards Paris, even as a hungry lion when he espies a stag or a wild goat upon the hills. But when Paris saw Menelaus spring out so boldly from the front rank of the Greeks, his heart quailed within him at the sight, and he shrank back amid the sheltering crowd of his comrades, even as a wayfaring man when he sees a deadly snake before him on the path. Hector sternly reproved him.

"Wretched Paris, that canst do nought but beguile women with thy fair face, would that thou hadst never been born, or hadst died unwedded, ere thou hadst brought shame upon us all. Well may the Greeks jeer at thee for a cowardly braggart. I know not how you ever could persuade brave men to follow you across the sea to steal another's bride. You have brought endless sorrow upon your father, your city, and your friends; and now your enemies rejoice, and you are covered with shame. No wonder you dared not meet brave Menelaus, else would you have learned the might of him whose wife you

stole. Indeed, were not the men of Troy
too forbearing, they would long ago have
stoned you to death, to requite you for the
evil you have wrought them."

Paris answered, " Hector, you have justly
blamed me. I cannot always be as brave
as you : yet if you wish me to dare the fight,
bid the Trojans and the Greeks sit down
upon the ground, and I in the midst of them
will fight bold Menelaus face to face, for
Helen and the spoil that I bore away. And
whichever of us two shall prove the better
man, let him take her and lead her home in
triumph. So shall you and the rest of the
Trojans dwell in peace, and the Greeks shall
return to their native Argos."

Thus spoke Paris, and Hector rejoiced at
his words. He forthwith proclaimed a truce,
made his men sit down, and bade Agamemnon
hold back the Greeks, while they two arranged
the terms of the combat. And soon, at the
bidding of a herald, King Priam himself came
down from Troy in a chariot driven by his
old friend and counsellor, Antenor. In the

open space between the two armies Priam
and Antenor alighted from their chariot,
and were met by Agamemnon and Odysseus,
the chiefs of the Greeks. The heralds mixed
some wine in a bowl, and led up to the
princes two lambs, which Priam had brought
in his chariot. Agamemnon drew his sword,
cut the wool from the heads of the lambs,
gave some of it to each of the chiefs, both
of the Greeks and of the Trojans, and then,
raising his hands to heaven, prayed aloud to
Father Zeus, and Helios the sun-god that
seeth all things, and to the gods of the nether
world that punish wicked men, to witness
the covenant.

"If," said he, "Menelaus fall by the hand
of Paris, then shall Paris keep both Helen
and the spoil, and all the other Greeks shall
return to their homes in peace. If Menelaus
slay Paris, then shall Troy give up both
Helen and the spoil, with fitting compensa-
tion for the wrong that has been done.
But if Paris fall, and then the Trojans shall
refuse to pay the forfeit due, I and the rest

will stay here and fight even unto the end."

He ceased, and with his sword cut the throats of the lambs, and poured the wine upon the ground, while all around prayed to Father Zeus, that whosoever might break the covenant, his heart's best blood might be poured upon the ground even as this wine.

After this, Priam remounted his chariot, and drove away to the breezy heights of Troy : for he had not the heart to stay, and see his darling son meet fierce Menelaus in battle.

Now Hector and Odysseus measured out the ground, and placed two lots in a helmet, for which of the two should first hurl his spear. Tall Hector himself, with eyes turned away, shook the helmet, and first sprang out the lot of Paris. Each champion now armed him for the fight, placed on his breast his corslet, on his legs his greaves, and on his head his helmet, with its tall nodding plume. Over their shoulders they placed the strap by

which their sword was slung, took in their
left hands their shields, of many a fold of the
tough bull's hide, and with their spears in
their right hands strode manfully to their
stations, while all around held their breath,
Greeks and Trojans alike, to see those two
fierce warriors, with deadly hate gleaming
from their eyes, making ready to fight.
First Paris hurled his spear. Menelaus
caught it fair upon his shield : but the point
was turned upon the brass of the shield, and
did not pierce it. Next Menelaus, with a
prayer to Zeus, dealt Paris so fell a stroke
with his spear, that it passed clean through
his shield, through his corslet, and just grazed
his side, yet made no wound. Menelaus
now drew his sword and smote Paris upon
the crest of his helmet. The sword flew to
shivers in his grasp, and Menelaus, looking
up to heaven, cried, "Father Zeus, it is but
in vain that I call upon thee, for now is my
sword broken in my hand, and my spear has
been hurled without wounding my foe."

As he spoke, he seized Paris by the horse-

hair plume of his helmet, wrenched it round,
and dragged him along towards the Greeks.
The strap of the helmet, by which it was
fastened under his chin, would have choked
Paris, and Menelaus would have won the
fight, had not Aphrodite caused the strap to
break, and snatched away her favourite from
death. Hidden in a cloud, she wafted him
away to Troy, to his own chamber, where,
in the arms of Helen, he consoled himself for
his defeat. Meanwhile Menelaus rushed
savagely among the crowd, seeking every-
where for the vanished Paris. Yet none of
all the Trojans could point him out to
Menelaus; not that they would have screened
him for any love they bore him, for all ab-
horred him because of the troubles he had
brought upon them. At last out spoke
great Agamemnon.

"Ye Trojans, Dardans, and allies. Menelaus is the victor. Wherefore give up to us
Helen and the spoil, with fitting compensa-
tion." Thus he spoke, and all the Greeks
cheered his words.

HOW HECTOR FOUGHT AJAX

CHAPTER V

How Hector fought Ajax

MEANWHILE Pallas Athênê, eager to break off the truce, came down among the Trojans in the likeness of Laodocus, a son of Antenor. She swiftly made her way to where stood Pandarus the archer, begirt by the trusty warriors whom he brought from the banks of the dark Æsepus. To him thus spoke the false Laodocus.

"Son of Lycaon, hearken to my counsel. If thou wilt shoot an arrow and slay Menelaus, great will be thy fame: and great thy reward also from Paris, when he shall hear that Menelaus is laid low. Shoot then, and pray to Phoebus Apollo that thy arrow may fly straight."

Thus spoke Athênê, and he, fool that he was, hearkened to her words. Straightway he strung his polished bow, made of the horns of a mountain ibex, which he himself, lurking in ambush, had shot through the breast as it came round the corner of a crag. Its head bore horns sixteen palms long, and these a workman had cunningly joined together, and tipped them at the ends with gold. Pandarus now fitted an arrow to the string, his trusty comrades the while holding their shields before him, lest the Greeks should see him aiming the arrow, and rush upon him before he could shoot the noble Menelaus. He chose a new arrow, vowed a goodly sacrifice to Apollo, drew the bowstring to his breast, and the iron head of the arrow to the bow, and then, when the great bow was strained into a circle, with a loud twang the eager arrow sped towards its mark.

Then, Menelaus, hadst thou surely fallen, had not Pallas Athênê marked the flight of the arrow, and guided it to where the sword-belt crossed the breastplate, and the stout girdle lay beneath it : yet through all these

the arrowhead piecred, and fast flowed the
dark blood over the fair skin of Menelaus,
as when a Lydian or Carian woman stains
a piece of ivory with crimson dye, to deck
the headgear of some warrior's steed.   At
the sight of the blood great Agamemnon
shuddered, and said, clasping his brother by the
hand :

" It was for thy death, then, that I made
the truce, which now the Trojans have so foully
broken !   They shall pay the penalty for this,
soon or late ; but sore will be my grief for
thee, my brother, if it be fated that thou
must die, and I must return with shame to
Argos : for well I know the Greeks will all
set sail for home, and we shall leave Helen as
a prize to Priam and the Trojans.   Thy
bones will rot in the land of Troy, thy life's
work left undone ; and some Trojan, as he
leaps upon the grave of bold Menelaus, will
boastfully say, ' Thus may Agamemnon ever
accomplish his desire upon his enemies.   He
led hither a mighty host, and now is gone
home empty-handed, leaving brave Menelaus

F

behind.' O may the earth open and cover my shame on that day."

Thus grieved Agamemnon : but Menelaus showed him that the barb of the arrow had not entered the wound, and that it was not mortal. Then Agamemnon bade Machaon, the physician, draw out the arrow and soothe the pain of the wound with healing herbs, which old Cheiron had given to Machaon's father, Asclepius, while he himself set the Greeks in battle-array, for the Trojans were making ready to charge. He visited every company of spearmen, and gave praise or blame to each. As he thus reviewed the host, he came to where the bold Cretans, round their king Idomeneus, were arming for the fight. " Well done," said he, " brave Idomeneus ; no prince hath more honour than thou, when the chiefs of the Greeks feast at my table. Up now, and prove thyself the warrior that thou art."

" Fear not for me," answered Idomeneus, " I will play my part. But do thou stir up the Greeks to fight, now that the truce is broken."

So Agamemnon passed on and came to
where the greater and the lesser Ajax stood
amid dark ranks of warriors, bristling with
spear and shield. Eager for battle the host
moved forward, like unto the black cloud which
the shepherd from his lofty crag sees sweeping
over the sea, dark as night, bringing with it
a hurricane of rain.

Well-pleased at the sight, Agamemnon
said to them:

"To you I need give no orders. You
know full well how to rouse the courage of
your followers. Would that all in our camp
were as brave: then should Priam's lofty
city soon be ours."

Thus saying, he passed on to where old
Nestor, the king of sandy Pylos, was setting
his men in order. He placed the chariots in
front, and the foot-soldiers behind, with the
worst troops between the two, so that they
were forced to fight even if they wished it
not. He bade the horsemen not press on
too far alone, nor yet fall back one by one,
but to drive forward in one body, and thrust

with their spears at the chariots of the foe-
men; for thus, he said, battles were won in the
days of old. Agamemnon's heart was glad
as he saw old Nestor thus busied, and he said :

" Would to heaven, old man, thy strength
were as great as thy spirit; but old age
weighs thee down: I would that some others
were as old as thou, and thou young again."

"Son of Atreus," replied Nestor cheerily,
"I too wish that I were now as young and
strong as when I slew Ereuthalion in single
fight, many a long year ago. Yet, aged as I
am, I can still go forth with the chariots and
direct the war."

Next Agamemnon came to where stood
Menestheus with the Athenians, and Odysseus
with his islanders. They had not heard the
call to battle, and knew not that the truce
was broken, but stood still, awaiting what
might befall. Agamemnon sharply rebuked
them, and said:

" Royal Menestheus, and thou, arch-de-
ceiver Odysseus, why stand you loitering here,
while others bear the brunt of battle ? You

ought to be foremost in fight, for you are
foremost at my table, and ever eat of the fat
and drink of the strong; yet here you stand
idle, while others pass before you to battle?"

Then Odysseus answered angrily:

" For shame, Agamemnon! How dare you
say that we shrink from battle? Whenever
the Trojans renew the war, you shall see,
if you care to see it, that the father of
Telemachus fights ever in the front rank. To
speak thus is foolishness."

Then Agamemnon owned to Odysseus
that he had spoken in haste, and that his
reproach was unjust. So he passed on to
where Diomedes, and Sthenelus, his comrade,
stood beside their chariots.

" Why so backward?" asked he, " why so
loth to join battle? Of a truth thy father
Tydeus was a brave man, for he alone, when
sent on an embassy to Thebes, challenged the
Thebans to wrestle, and overcame them all;
and when they in anger laid an ambush for
him, he slew all save one, whom he sent to
bear the tidings to Thebes. So brave a man

was he, but he hath begotten a son who falls
short of him in battle, although he be a better
speaker in the assembly."

Thus spoke Agamemnon, and Diomedes
modestly hung down his head, nor dared to
answer the great chief of the Greeks; but
Sthenelus, the son of Capaneus, boldly said:

"Say not so, Agamemnon. We are better
men by far than our fathers were, for we, by
the aid of Ares, took seven-gated Thebes, with
only a small force, after our fathers had failed,
through their own boastful folly, with a great
one. So never compare their deeds with ours."

"Be silent, friend," said Diomedes. "Agamemnon is right when he bids us make ready
for battle, and I bear him no malice for what
he has said."

As, when a strong west wind blows, the
waves first rear their crests far out at sea, and
then, growing ever longer and heavier as
they draw nigher to the land, break with a
thunderous roar upon the beach, and toss the
spray high above the tall cliffs of the shore,
even so did the Greeks that day roll unceas-

ingly onward against the hosts of Troy. Man to man and lance to lance they fought; and dread was the clash of shield against shield, the shouts of the warriors, and the groans of the fallen, while beneath their feet the plain of Troy ran red with blood. First Antilochus struck Echepolus, a Trojan warrior, through the temples with his spear. He fell dead, and Elephenor of Euboea caught him by the feet, hoping to drag him away and spoil him of his armour; but bold Agenor marked Elephenor as he stooped, and thrust his brazen spear into his unguarded side. Over their corpses the fight waxed hot. Ajax laid low Simoisius, so named because he was born on the banks of reedy Simois. But as young Leucus, the faithful comrade of Odysseus, was in act to bear away the body, Antiphus, a son of Priam, drove a spear deep into his groin, that he fell dead, across dead Simoisius. Then Odysseus, grieving for his friend, hurled his spear. He missed Antiphus, but struck Democoon through the forehead, and closed his eyes in death.

At this the Trojan chiefs, nay, Hector himself began to give way ; but Apollo shouted loudly to them—

" Fight, brave Trojans, flinch not from the Greeks. Their flesh is not of iron, nor their sinews of wire, that no steel can wound them. Remember, Achilles wars not for them now, but sits idle beside his ships, nursing his wrath."

Then did Pallas Athênê give strength and courage to Diomedes, that he won more fame than all the rest of the Greeks. His helmet flashed in the sunlight, like the bright star that shines in harvest time. First he struck down Phegeus, the son of Dares, who was driving a chariot with his brother Idaeus. When Idaeus saw his brother fall, he leaped from the chariot and fled, while Diomedes caught the horses, and bade his comrades drive them away to his own tent. Now the Greeks drove back the Trojans. Agamemnon, Idomeneus, and Menelaus, each laid low a chief; while Meriones slew Phereclus, the cunning workman, who in an evil

hour had built the ships for Paris. But no
man could say of Diomedes whether he
belonged to the Greek or to the Trojan host,
for he dashed across the plain hither and
thither, like to a mountain torrent in flood,
that bears away bridges and hedges in its
wild career. After a while, Pandarus shot
an arrow, that struck him on the right
shoulder, but not so was Diomedes quelled.
Sthenelus drew forth the arrow, and Pallas
closed the wound, and eased him of his pain.
Then Æneas, seeing what havoc Diomedes
wrought, took Pandarus into his chariot—
for Pandarus had come on foot to Troy—
and they two went to meet Diomedes, and
try to check his fierce onset. Æneas drove
the horses, for they knew his voice, and
Pandarus, when they drew near, hurled his
spear full at Diomedes. But he, though far
away from help, scorned to fall back. The
spear of Pandarus pierced through his shield,
and through his breastplate. For a moment
Pandarus thought him wounded, but the
next instant the spear of Diomedes whizzed

through the air. It smote Pandarus beneath the eye, crashed through his teeth, and felled him to the earth a corpse. Down sprang Æneas to defend his body, but Diomedes hurled a great stone, which would have slain Æneas too, had not his goddess-mother seen the peril of her son and snatched him from his doom. But nought could stop Diomedes that day: men said that he levelled his spear against Aphrodite herself. So fiercely did he rage, that ere long Helenus, the Trojan seer, bade Hector go back to Troy, and bid the matrons and elders kneel at the shrine of Athênê, and pray that her wrath might be turned away.

When Hector came near to the fig-tree which stands before the Scaean gate, the wives and daughters of the Trojans came out to meet him, eager to hear how their husbands and brothers had fared in the battle. He bade them pray to the gods for victory, and passed on into the city. His mother came to meet him, bearing a goblet full of wine, yet he would not taste it, but bade her lead the

matrons to the shrine of Pallas Athênê, and
lay a rich shawl on the knees of the goddess,
if haply thus her wrath might be turned
away. Thence Hector went to the house of
Paris, and sternly called upon him to dally
no longer with Helen, but to come forth and
fight like a man. While Paris was putting
on his armour, Hector went to his own
home, but he did not find his wife Andromache within—for she was gone, with her
little son Astyanax, to the loftiest tower of
Troy, to overlook the battle. Soon he met
her, and silently smiled as he gazed upon his
son, but Andromache with tearful eyes hung
upon his arm, and said:

"My hero, thy great heart will be thy
death. Thou hast no pity for this dear child,
nor for me, soon to be thy widow—for all the
Greeks will fall upon thee and slay thee: but
for me, when I am bereft of thee, it will be
best by far to die. No comfort will be left
me then, but only endless sorrow. I have no
father, nor mother, for Achilles slew my father
what time he took our city of Thebe under

Placos. He slew him, but stripped him not, for he reverenced the dead: wherefore he burned him in his armour, and heaped a mound above him, where now tall elm-trees grow. I had seven brothers, and all the seven perished in one day, at the hands of fierce Achilles. My mother he set free for a ransom, but she died of grief. So, Hector, thou art all in all to me, mother, father, brethren : thou, my wedded love. Show then some pity for me : stay here upon this tower, and make not thy child an orphan, and thy wife a widow. Range the host here, beside the fig-tree, where the city is most easy to assault, and where the walls are lowest. For thrice already have the bravest Greeks attacked it here, the two Ajaces and Idomeneus, and the two sons of Atreus and Diomedes, either guided by some oracle, or led by their own fiery spirit."

Thus she spoke, weeping bitterly; and Hector replied:

" Indeed, wife, I too think of all this, and grieve : but I should blush to meet the men

of Troy, and the Trojan ladies with their
trailing robes, were I to skulk, cowardlike,
away from battle. Besides, I have no wish
to stay behind, for I have learned ever to be
bold, and lead the van in fight, as becomes
my father's son. Full well indeed I know
in my inmost heart, that the day shall surely
come when stately Troy shall be levelled with
the ground, and Priam and all Priam's sons
shall be slain. Yet not the thought of the
fall of Troy, or of King Priam, or of my
mother Hecuba, or my many brave brethren,
all lying low in the dust, moves me so much
as the thought of thee, robbed of thy liberty,
and led away captive by some brass-harnessed
Greek, to weave at his loom in Argos, or to
draw water from the founts of Hypereia or
Messeis for a strange master. Perchance on
that day some who see thee weeping will say,
' This was the wife of Hector, who fought best
of all the Trojans when the battle waxed hot
round their wall.' Thus will they speak,
and thy grief will be renewed for the loss of
him who might have saved thee from slavery.

But may I die, and be buried deep beneath the earth, before I hear thy shrieks, and see thee led away."

So spoke Hector, and stretched forth his arms to take his child, but the babe shrank from him, scared by his glancing helm and nodding horse-hair plume. Both parents smiled, and Hector took off his helmet, and laid it, all glittering, on the ground. Then he took the child, and dandled it in his arms, praying thus the while to Zeus and all the Immortals.

"Grant, Zeus, and all ye gods, that this my boy may be, like me, the foremost man in Troy, that men may say, 'This youth is braver far than his father,' when they see him, having slain a foeman, carrying home his spoils from battle to rejoice his mother's heart."

Thus saying, he put back the child upon its mother's breast, and she clasped it to her, smiling through her tears. Hector bade her farewell, and strode away to the battle, while she with faltering steps, and shedding scalding

tears, went home to Hector's house ; and all
her maidens wept with her.

Now Hector and Paris, their bright arms
flashing like the sun in his splendour, returned
to where the Greeks and Trojans fought.
Soon each slew a warrior, as did also Glaucus,
the son of Hippolochus, their Lycian ally.
Then Pallas and Apollo, grieved at so much
slaughter, put a thought into the mind of
Helenus the seer, that he bade Hector
proclaim a truce, and challenge some Greek
to single fight. When both sides had sat
down, Hector said aloud:

" Hearken, Trojans and Greeks. It did
not please the gods to let our late truce endure. But now, as all the chiefs of the Greeks
are here, let one of them, whosoever dares,
come forth and fight with me alone. If he
prevail and slay me with his spear, then let
him strip off my armour, and bear it away
to his ship, but give back my body to my
friends for burial. But if I slay him, with
Apollo's aid, then will I hang his arms in the
temple of Apollo, and give back his corpse,

that ye may bury it, and heap a mound above it by the side of the broad Hellespont. And perchance, in days to come, some man will say, as he sails in his gallant ship over the dark blue sea, ' Yonder stands the tomb of one who died long ago, whom the brave Hector slew in fair fight.' Thus men will say : and my fame will endure for ever."

So spoke Hector : and all the Greeks sat dumb, fearing to meet so fierce a warrior alone. Menelaus indeed would fain have fought him, but his brother Agamemnon held him back, else had he surely died, for even Achilles himself was loth to meet Hector in single fight. After a long silence, old Nestor rose and spoke.

" Alas for Hellas," said he, " that we should be shamed thus. How would the ancient Peleus grieve to hear how Hector by his challenge has cowed us all. He would raise his hands to Heaven and pray that his soul might go down to Hades beneath the earth for very shame. Would that I had now the strength of my youthful days,

when the men of Pylos fought against
the bold Arcadians beside the swift stream
of Celadon, what time brave Ereuthalion
stepped forth from their ranks, and challenged
all our chiefs to single fight. None dared
accept his challenge save I, the youngest of
them all. I fought with him that day, and
slew him. O would that to-day my strength
were the same; then should Hector soon
find a champion to fight for Hellas ; but ye,
the bravest of the Greeks, flinch from the
fight."

Thus bitterly spoke Nestor ; but at his
rebuke rose nine warriors, Agamemnon,
Diomedes, the two Ajaces, Idomeneus and
his faithful Meriones, Eurypylus, Thoas the
son of Andraemon, and Odysseus. All these
offered to fight with Hector. Each marked
a lot, and put it in Agamemnon's helmet, and
he shook it till one lot came out, while all
around prayed:

"Grant, Father Zeus, that the lot may
fall either on Ajax, or on Diomedes, or on
the wealthy lord of Mycenae himself."

While they prayed, there sprang out the lot of Ajax, for which they had hoped. Ajax knew the token which he had put into the helmet, and rejoiced that he was chosen to meet Hector in fight. Proudly he strode forward, and all the Trojans shuddered when they marked his huge bulk and broad shoulders. Even Hector's heart beat quicker, but there was no escape for him, the challenger.

"Now, Hector," said Ajax, "you shall learn in single fight that there are many stout warriors left in our host, even though Achilles be away."

"Ajax," answered Hector, "seek not to frighten me, as though I were a child or a woman, unskilled in war. I know well how to sway hither and thither my shield of the tough bull's hide, and how to fight in chariots or on foot. And now I will slay thee, if I may, not by stealth, but in open fight."

So saying he hurled his long spear, but could not pierce the mighty shield of Ajax. Ajax then in turn hurled his spear at Hector.

It pierced his shield, made its way through
the well-wrought breastplate beneath, and
even tore the linen tunic on his breast, but
Hector, stooping, avoided the point of the
spear. Each now dragged out his weapon,
and fell fiercely upon his foe. Hector struck
Ajax full upon his shield, but the blunted
spear-point would not pass through, and
turned back. Ajax drove his spear through
Hector's shield, and grazed his neck. Blood
followed the stroke, but Hector, undismayed,
caught up a great stone which lay near, black,
rough, and huge. He hurled the stone at
Ajax, and struck his shield with a fearful
clatter. Ajax now took up a much bigger
stone, like a millstone, and hurled it at
Hector. It crushed in his shield, and
Hector's knees gave way beneath him at
that fell stroke : yet Apollo quickly raised
him up again. And now they each drew
their swords, and would have fought hand
to hand, had not the heralds, the sacred
messengers of gods and men, Talthybius
the Greek, and Idaeus the Trojan, stepped

forward with their long staves, and forbade them to fight any more, as darkness was coming on apace.

"Fight no longer," said they; "both of you are dear to Zeus who sitteth above the clouds, and both are warriors bold. But now it is night; and the night we must obey."

Ajax answered, "Idaeus, say this first to Hector. He challenged me to fight, and he must first offer to cease : then will I obey him."

Then Hector said :

"Ajax, you are brave and strong, and fight best of all the Greeks with the spear. Let us now cease from fighting, for indeed it is now dark. I will go home to Troy, and gladden the hearts of the Trojans, and do thou gladden thy comrades beside the ships. Another day we will fight, until Zeus shall give one or the other of us the victory. But let us to-night part good friends, and give presents one to another, that all men may say, 'They fought bravely, in single fight, and then parted friends.'"

Thus he spoke ; and in an evil hour for
each, they gave one another presents.   Hector
gave Ajax a sword, and Ajax gave Hector
a belt studded with plates of silver.   So they
parted.

That   night   Agamemnon   feasted   Ajax
royally in his tent, for the brave deeds he
had done ; and on the morrow the Greeks
and the Trojans gathered up the bodies of
the slain, and bewailed the valiant dead.

HOW HECTOR TRIED TO BURN
THE SHIPS

CHAPTER VI

How Hector tried to burn the Ships

W HEN the Trojans next came forth to
battle, they drove the Greeks quite
back to their fenced camp. Old Nestor was
nearly cut off, for Paris shot one of his horses,
and while the old man tried to cut the harness with his sword, Hector was fast driving
towards him. Nothing could have saved
Nestor, had Hector come within reach of
him ; but just in time Diomedes, driving the
swift horses which he had taken from Æneas,
took up the good old man in his chariot and
bore him away in safety. Diomedes withal
hurled his spear at Hector, and though he
missed him, yet he slew his charioteer ; so
while Hector sought for some one else to

drive his chariot, Diomedes and Nestor reached the camp unhurt. That night the Trojans were so bold, and felt so sure of victory that they would not go back into Troy, but lighted great fires and lay all night on the open plain, ready to storm the camp on the morrow. All the Greeks felt anxious and disheartened, fearing what the morrow might bring forth, lest the Trojans should win the day, and break through the wall of the camp, and cut the host to pieces beside the ships. Then said Nestor :

" It were well that one should go forth, if any here be bold enough, to play the spy upon the Trojans in their camp, and learn what they intend for the morrow. If any one dared do this, he would do good service, and win great renown."

Then answered brave Diomedes :

"Nestor, I dare to go. But let some trusty comrade come with me : for two going together can keep a sharper look-out, and can more readily guard themselves from harm."

Upon this, many chiefs offered to go with

Diomedes; and out of them all he chose
Odysseus, for he knew his ready wit and
dauntless spirit. Diomedes and Odysseus now
put on helmets without either crest or plume.
Thrasymedes gave Diomedes a sword, and
Meriones gave Odysseus a bow and arrows,
for they had come from their tents unarmed.
Then they two set out through the night.
They had not gone far from the gates of the
camp before Odysseus saw some one moving
near them, and pointed him out to Diomedes.

"See," said he, "hither comes some one.
He must mean either to rob the slain, or to
play the spy upon our camp. Let us step
aside out of the path, and let him pass by us
a little way; then will we rush upon him
unawares and catch him, or, if he outruns us,
we can drive him towards our ships, and cut
him off from his own people."

So they two crouched down beside the
path, and let the stranger pass; but when
he was distant about a stone's throw, they
rushed upon him. At the sound of their
footsteps he stopped, for he thought that

Hector, who had sent him forth, might perchance have sent messengers from the camp to bid him return; but when they came within a spear's length he knew them for foes, and ran swiftly from them, while they chased him, even as two hounds that run on the track of a deer. But when he came close to the camp of the Greeks, Diomedes shouted to him to stop, and threw his spear so as just to pass over his shoulder without hitting him. Then he stopped, and stood panting, with chattering teeth, till they came up and seized him.

"Spare my life," begged he; "I can pay you a goodly ransom, for I have store of gold and silver, and my father will give much treasure if he hears that I live." Odysseus answered him:

"Be of good cheer, and think not of death, but tell us, how came you here alone, in the dark night, when all men sleep? Was it to rob the slain, or did Hector send you to play the spy upon us?"

Then Dolon, for that was his name, said:

"Hector beguiled me by a mighty bribe to

come and see whether your camp was guarded
or no, and whether you meant to fight on the
morrow, or to betake you to your ships and
flee away. He promised me the horses and
the chariot of Achilles as my reward if I
would do this."

Odysseus answered with scorn :

"A noble reward indeed, the horses of
Achilles! Few mortals can harness them
or drive them, save only goddess - born
Achilles himself. But tell me, where is
Hector? whereabouts lie the Trojans and
their allies, and what are their counsels?"

Then Dolon said :

"Hector and all the rest of the chiefs are
met in counsel at the tomb of Ilus. No
guards protect the camp. A watch is indeed
kept around the fires, but the allies sleep care-
lessly, and trust their safety to the Trojans.
Next to the sea lie the Carians, Leleges, and
Paeonians, while near Thymbra are the Lycians
under Glaucus and Sarpedon. But why ask
about these? If you have a mind to fall upon
our camp, farthest off of all lie the Thracians,

who have but just come, and in the midst of them sleeps their king, Rhesus, the son of Eioneus, a godlike man. His horses and chariot are beyond compare, and his armour is all of red gold, a wonder to be seen. But now let me go, or else take me to your ships as a captive, and see if my words prove not true."

Diomedes turned sternly upon Dolon, and said:

"Think not to escape, though you have told us good tidings. If we let you go, you may again draw near our camp, either as a secret spy or open foe: but if I slay you now, you nevermore will cause us trouble."

As he spoke, he drove his sword through Dolon's throat, and Odysseus took Dolon's cap, wolf-skin cloak, and bow, hid them beneath a tamarisk bush, and set a mark on the spot with broken twigs, that he might know the place again.

Then Odysseus and Diomedes set forth again, and soon they came to where lay the newly-come Thracians, without guards, sunk heavily in sleep. They lay in their ranks, each

man with his arms by his side, and their horses
stood ready harnessed, tied to their chariots.
In the midst lay King Rhesus himself, and
beside him stood his noble horses.   Odysseus
pointed him out to Diomedes, and straightway
Diomedes fell upon the sleeping Thracians
with his sword, even as a hungry lion when
he bursts by night into a full sheepfold.   As
he stabbed them, Odysseus seized the bodies
by the feet, and drew them out of the way,
for he feared that the horses of Rhesus would
not step over the corpses, above all when
driven by strange hands.   Twelve of the
Thracians Diomedes slew, and the thirteenth
was King Rhesus himself, who lay fast asleep,
wrestling with an evil dream.   Meanwhile
Odysseus loosed the horses, brought them
under the yoke, gathered up the reins, and
softly whistled to Diomedes to come with
him, lest some of the Thracians should wake,
and all their toil be in vain.   Diomedes leapt
up beside him, and Odysseus with his bow,
for he could not find the whip, drove the
horses swiftly to the camp of the Greeks.

Rosy morn was breaking over the peaks of Mount Ida when Odysseus and Diomedes drove proudly up to the gate of the camp. At the gate Nestor met them, and bade them welcome home.

"Hail," said he, "brave warriors: but tell me, whence have you got these horses? Old though I be, I fight ever in the front rank, and I know the horses of all the Trojan princes; but never have I seen such noble steeds as these. Surely some god must have given them to you, for both of you, I know, are dear to the gods."

Odysseus answered him:

"The gods, Nestor, if they chose, could easily give us finer horses than these. But these, about which you ask, are of Thracian breed, and Diomedes hath slain their lord, and twelve of his comrades with him."

So they drove into the camp rejoicing; and Agamemnon mustered the host and led it boldly forth to do battle with the Trojans. No man that day had more glory than Agamemnon, the son of Atreus: for he fought

far before the rest, and laid low many a
proud Trojan, and beat back their host, until
about mid-day he was struck through the
right hand by Koon, Antenor's eldest son.
Koon would fain have dragged away the
body of his brother Iphidamas, who dwelt at
Percote, and whom Agamemnon had slain :
but as he stooped to raise the corpse, Agamemnon sprang fiercely upon him, and with
one thrust of his spear laid him dead beside
his brother.

For a time Agamemnon fought on, but
ere long the pain of his wound forced him
to mount his chariot, and drive home to
the camp. Then Hector pressed forward.
Diomedes and Odysseus, wearied with their
foray of the night, had only just come into
the battle when Hector met them. Diomedes
struck Hector such a blow on the helmet
with his spear that Hector turned faint and
dizzy, and was forced to fall back for a while :
but Paris shot Diomedes in the ankle, and
made him too leave the battle. So Odysseus
was left all alone, and the Trojans gathered

H

round him, even as dogs and men gather round a wild boar, who stands at bay, champing the foam from his tusks, and they, bold though they be, dare not venture within his reach. So stood Odysseus, and struck down Charops, the son of Hippasus; but Socus, the brother of Charops, dealt Odysseus a grievous wound in the side. Odysseus felt that his wound was not mortal, and as Socus turned to flee, darted his spear through him from back to breast. Yet Odysseus, wounded and alone, must surely have fallen, had he not shouted aloud for help, and been heard afar off by great Ajax and Menelaus, who came up and rescued him. And now, as most of their chiefs were wounded, the Greeks turned and fled. Back to the camp they fled, and onward pressed the exulting Trojans. Alone, Ajax on the one flank, and brave old Idomeneus on the other, strove to stay the flight, but at last they too were swept away by the fleeing host.

From the prow of his tall ship Achilles watched the fortune of the battle. As he

saw one chief after another return wounded
to the camp, and at last saw the whole line
of the Greeks give way, he said to his friend
Patroclus:

"Methinks ere long the Greeks will kneel
as suppliants before my feet; for their need is
sore.   But haste thee, Patroclus, and learn
who this is whom Nestor is bringing back
wounded in his chariot.   Seen from behind,
he looks like Machaon the physician: but
the horses galloped past me so fast that I
could not see his face."

Patroclus ran quickly to the tent of Nestor,
where he found the old warrior drinking
a goblet of Pramnian wine, mixed with
grated cheese of goat's milk and barley meal,
with an onion for a relish.   By his side sat
Machaon, the wounded physician, while the
servants were warming water to wash his
wounds withal.   Patroclus, when he saw
Machaon, would have gone back to Achilles
forthwith, but Nestor said to him:

"What cares Achilles how many of the
Greeks are hurt?   Does he not know that Dio-

medes, Odysseus, Agamemnon himself, and
Eurypylus, have all been wounded, and now I
myself have brought another, Machaon here,
whom Paris has shot with an arrow in the
shoulder? Would that I were young again :
soon would I do some brave deed. But do
thou, Patroclus, pray Achilles, if he will not
come forth himself, to lend thee his armour,
and come forth thyself in his likeness, if
perchance the men of Troy may be scared by
the sight. Thou and the Myrmidons, fresh
and unwearied, might well drive them back."

So spoke Nestor, and Patroclus sped back to
the tent of Achilles, while Nestor drew forth
the arrow from Machaon's shoulder, washed
the wound, and bound healing herbs upon it.

Meanwhile the Greeks and the Trojans
were fighting hand to hand: for the ditch
and the strong rampart, set close with stakes,
no longer kept out the foe. Down to earth
leaped the Trojan chiefs from their chariots,
and onwards they pressed towards the gates
in five companies, one led by Hector and
wise Polydamas, one by Paris, the third by

Helenus, Deiphobus, and Asius, the son of Hyrtacus, the fourth by Æneas, and the fifth by Glaucus and Sarpedon, the princes of the Lycians.

Asius charged at one of the gates with his chariot, but Idomeneus drove him back amid a shower of darts. But Hector, albeit Polydamas would fain have held him back, fiercely assaulted another gate, and Sarpedon said to Glaucus:

"Cousin Glaucus, why do the Lycians honour us with the highest seats at feasts, the largest messes of meat, and the fullest cups of wine; why have we so goodly a heritage of cornfield and vineyard beside the stream of Xanthus, if we be not foremost in fight? Since man must die, and can die but once, let us on, and win glory for ourselves, or let others earn it by our fall."

So saying, he assailed the wall, and though Menestheus of Athens, who defended it, called Ajax and Teucer the archer to his aid, Sarpedon made his way to the battlements. Great Ajax hurled a stone, which slew a

comrade of Sarpedon, and Teucer wounded
Glaucus with an arrow; but Sarpedon tore
down the stakes of the parapet, and laid open
a great breach, through which the Lycians
strove to force their way. Yet so firmly did
the Greeks within stand their ground, that
none could pass through until Hector, seizing
a great stone, such as not two men could lift,
such as men now are, cast it against the gate
before him. The blow burst all the fasten-
ings of the gate, snapped the stout bar behind
it, and, through the passage thus made, the
Trojans stormed in, while the Greeks fled to
their ships in headlong rout. At the ships a
few of the leaders rallied. Idomeneus and
his faithful Meriones checked the Trojans,
for Meriones met Deiphobus and would have
wounded him had not his spear broken in his
grasp, while Idomeneus slew Othryoneus,
who was but lately come to the war, for the
love of fair Cassandra, the most beauteous of
Priam's daughters. Him now Idomeneus
slew; and when Asius, the son of Hyrtacus,
came up to drag away the corpse, Idomeneus

dealt him a stab in the neck with his spear, and felled great Asius to the ground, even as shipwrights fell some tall pine-tree upon the mountains, to form the keel of a great ship. Yet soon Deiphobus, Æneas, and many more Trojan warriors overpowered Idomeneus, and forced him to give way. Hector now called aloud for fire, and himself with a torch tried to set light to the ship of Protesilaus: yet for a long while he could not, for great Ajax stood on the bows of the ship wielding a huge pole, such as is used to work ships in shallow water, while Teucer, from beneath his brother's shield, unceasingly shot his arrows at the Trojans.

Patroclus, after returning to Achilles, had busied himself in tending the hurts of Eurypylus of Hypereia, whom he had met on his way, with his thigh pierced by an arrow. But after a while, when he saw a pillar of black smoke arise from the ship of Protesilaus, he could no longer bear to remain quiet and see Hector burn the fleet. Achilles himself refused to stir to help the Greeks, remembering the wrong which their chief had done him; and he knew well that he could defend his own tent and his own ship from Hector, however fiercely he might rage. Yet Patroclus begged so hard to be allowed to help his comrades, that at last Achilles lent him his own armour, and bade him lead the Myrmidons to the rescue; but he straitly charged Patroclus to do no more than save the ships, and drive the foe out of the camp, and when he had done so, to return, and not to fight with the Trojans in the open plain.

It was high time. Ajax had fought till he was weary, and his left arm could scarce support the weight of his great shield. Overwhelmed by the darts of the Trojans, which rang without ceasing upon his well-wrought helmet and shield, he was forced to give way, and the ship of Protesilaus was already in a blaze, when, clad in the well-known armour of Achilles, glittering like the sun in his splendour, Patroclus led the gallant Myrmidons into the thickest of the fight. There he slew Pyraechmes, the chief of the

Paeonians, and put his followers to flight.
As the breeze rolls away the dark wreaths of
mist which have gathered round a mountain,
and every peak and crag, and the blue vault
of heaven above appears again, to gladden
the shepherd's heart, even so did Patroclus
roll back the Trojan host from the burning
ships of the Greeks. Yet the Trojans did
not flee panic-stricken, but fought stoutly,
though forced to give way. Then were
done great deeds of arms. Patroclus and
Menelaus each slew a Trojan chief, while
Nestor's two sons, Antilochus and Thrasymedes, laid low two comrades of Sarpedon.
Nor were Meriones and Idomeneus backward
in the fight, but all together drove back the
Trojans with much slaughter over the rampart and through the ditch of the camp.
Patroclus, driving the immortal steeds of
Achilles, made for Hector himself, but though
unable to come up with him, he marked his
path by a dreadful line of corpses. Sarpedon,
seeing what havoc Patroclus wrought, called
to his Lycians to rally, and himself met

Patroclus face to face. Together rushed the two champions like two fierce vultures, and Father Zeus himself sorrowed for his beloved son, doomed to fall. Sarpedon struck dead Pedasus, the horse which Achilles had won at Lyrnessus; but Automedon the charioteer cut the reins and harness, and while Sarpedon hurled a second spear in vain, Patroclus smote him through the body just below the heart. Mortally wounded, brave Sarpedon fell to the ground: yet, as he fell, he cried to his comrade Glaucus to bring up the Lycians and bear off his body, and not let him fall into the hands of the Greeks.

Now Patroclus leaped down to the earth, and drew out his spear from the corpse of Sarpedon. Glaucus had heard Sarpedon's dying cry for help, and seizing his wounded arm, which Teucer had pierced with an arrow, he prayed to Apollo to heal the wound. His prayer was heard, and the god stanched the blood, and took away the pain. Then Glaucus was glad, and called first to the Lycians, and then to Hector and the other Trojan chiefs not to leave Sarpedon, nor let his body be cast to the dogs, but to rally round it and bear it away. Patroclus on his side brought up Ajax and Meriones, and a dreadful battle raged over the corpse. On brazen helm and shield the heavy strokes rung like the blows of a woodman's axe in the forest, and soon not the sharpest-sighted man could have recognised Sarpedon, covered as he was with broken weapons, blood, and dust from head to foot. Round him the warriors thronged even as the flies in spring-time round the frothing milk-pails, while from above Father Zeus looked down upon the slaughter, mourning for the fate of his son, and meditating evil against Patroclus who had slain him.

HOW PATROCLUS LOST THE
ARMS OF ACHILLES

CHAPTER VII

How Patroclus lost the Arms of Achilles

YET Father Zeus was minded that Patroclus should bear back the Trojans, and he sent panic among them, while at the same time he said to Phoebus Apollo:

"Go quickly, good Phoebus, drag away Sarpedon from amid yonder throng of spears. Wash his body in the river, anoint it with ambrosia, wrap it in immortal robes, and give it over to Sleep and Death, that they may swiftly bear it to his own fair land of Lycia, that his brethren and friends may bury him there, and raise a mound and a pillar over his grave."

So Phoebus did as he was commanded; but meanwhile Patroclus had stripped the rich

armour from Sarpedon's body, and sent it back
to his own tent. Patroclus now dashed forward, and none could stand before him. Ten
of the Trojans, one after another, fell beneath
his spear. In sooth he would that day have
taken the lofty-gated city of Troy, had not
Apollo himself stood upon one of the towers.
Thrice did Patroclus essay to mount the wall:
and thrice Apollo with his own immortal hand
thrust back his glittering shield; but when
he came on for the fourth time with more
than mortal strength, the Archer-God sternly
spoke:

"Back, gallant Patroclus! Not by thee, nor
even by Achilles, who is mightier far than thou,
do the Fates decree that Troy shall be won."

Meanwhile Hector stood beside his chariot
at the Scaean gate, musing whether he should
try any more to fight in the plain, or call back
the host to seek the shelter of the city walls.
Unto him came Apollo, in the likeness of
one of his comrades, and bade him go forth
again. "Would to heaven," quoth he, "that
I were as strong and brave as thou. Sorely

should I rue the missing of such a noble
chance. Fall boldly upon Patroclus, and
perchance Apollo may help thee to win the
day." On hearing his words, Hector straightway drove his steeds to meet Patroclus.
Patroclus leaped to the ground, with his
spear in his left hand, while with his right he
hurled a great stone, and struck Cebriones,
the driver of Hector's chariot, full on the
forehead. The jagged mass crushed in his
eyebrows, broke the bone, and felled him
headlong from the car. Then Patroclus,
jeering at his somersault, sprang upon the
body. Hector also leaped from his car, and
they fought one another hand to hand over
Cebriones, who never would drive chariot
again, but lay low in the dust, his mighty limbs
stretched out in the death-agony. Neither
side now thought of flight; javelins and arrows
flew thick and fast over Cebriones, and Patroclus fiercely pressed on his foe. But death
was near him. Apollo smote him, and he
reeled dizzy beneath the stroke. His helmet
fell to the ground—never before was that proud

helmet rolled in the mire, for, till that day, it decked the head of Achilles himself. Seeing how Patroclus stood bewildered, Euphorbus, the son of Panthous, struck him between the shoulders ; yet the hurt was not unto death, and Euphorbus did not dare to stand his ground, and meet Patroclus face to face. But Hector, when he saw Patroclus wounded, came forward, thrust his spear through his side, and felled him to the ground.

Thus did Patroclus, after all his mighty deeds of arms, fall at last by Hector's spear. As he lay, Hector exulted over him, saying—

"Patroclus, it was but now that you boasted that you would sack our lofty city, and bear our Trojan dames away captive to Greece; but you shall fatten the region-kites here where you lie. Little good hath the son of Peleus done you when he sent you forth to fight with me. Poor fool! I trow he bade you not return before you had laid the valiant Hector low."

Patroclus faintly made reply, for the hand of death was upon him, "Hector, it is now thy turn to boast, for the gods have delivered me into thy hand. Little would I fear thee on a fair field; but to-day Phoebus Apollo first smote me, and then Euphorbus. Thou camest but third; and I tell thee, moreover, that thy life shall not endure for long, but soon will Achilles slay thee before the Scaean gate."

Thus speaking he died, and his soul flitted away to the shadows of the nether world, wailing over the youth and strength that it left behind, cut off untimely ere its thread of life was fully spun. Hector would fain have laid his hands on the chariot as well, but Automedon swiftly drove away the immortal steeds.

Now Menelaus marked the fall of Patroclus, and quickly ran up, and held over his bleeding body the bright orb of his shield, while with his spear he menaced death to any that should seek to drive him away. But Euphorbus too had marked Patroclus for his own, and came forward boldly, saying—

"Brave Menelaus, fall back; leave the corpse

and the armour; for I was the first Trojan
who struck Patroclus: wherefore let me gain
glory by his fall."

Fiercely answered Menelaus:

"Indeed, the sons of Panthous are brave in
their own esteem.   Yet nought availed Hy-
perenor his youth and might, when he met
me, and said that of all the Greeks I was the
feeblest warrior.   He never returned to his
home, and never shall you return if you dare
to match yourself with me.   But stand back,
I warn you, lest my spear lay you low."

Thus spoke Menelaus: but Euphorbus
waxed hot with wrath when he remembered
his brother, whom Menelaus had slain, and
he thought that, could he cut off Menelaus's
head and carry it to his parents, it would be
some solace to them in their grief.   He
hurled his spear at Menelaus, but could not
pierce his shield, for the spear-point turned
back, and Menelaus, leaping forward, struck
his spear through Euphorbus's mouth and
throat, that it pierced right through his neck.
Down fell Euphorbus with a heavy thud, and

his armour rattled as he fell. His fair hair,
bound with a golden net, was befouled with
blood and mire, and he lay like some young
fruit-tree which a man has planted in his
orchard and nursed with care, till, just when
its branches are white with blossom, a hurricane tears it up by the roots and lays it low
upon the ground. Even so lay Euphorbus,
beautiful in death, while Menelaus pounced
upon him and stripped him, of his arms,
even as a lion pounces upon the fattest heifer
of the herd, and laps her blood. Though
many dogs and herdsmen clamour around,
none dares disturb the lion at his feast, and
no Trojan was there so bold as to meet the
wrathful Menelaus face to face. He would
surely have gained the arms and borne them
away, had not Apollo warned Hector no longer
to pursue the horses of Achilles, but to lead
all the chiefs to attack Menelaus and save
Euphorbus from him. Unwillingly then did
Menelaus leave the corpse of Patroclus,
ofttimes turning about and facing his foes,
until he saw great Ajax afar off. Menelaus

loudly called him to his aid, and they two
then returned to the fray.   Meanwhile
Hector had stripped the armour from the
body of Patroclus, and was dragging it away,
but when Ajax came, Hector dropped the
corpse and fell back.   Glaucus railed bitterly
at him for a coward; but Hector went back
only a little space, stripped off his own
armour, and put on that of Achilles, the
glorious armour which the gods gave to
Peleus on his wedding day.   Then, thus
arrayed, he hastened back to the fight.
Long they fought, and bravely; but such a
hedge of spears now girt the corpse of Patroclus, that no Trojan could reach to where
he lay.   Backward and forward rocked the
battle, and hard toiled either side, the Greeks
hoping to bear away the body to their camp,
the Trojans hoping to cast it to the dogs.

Meanwhile Achilles stood beside his tall
ships, overlooking the battle.   Full of gloomy
forebodings he said to himself—

" Woe is me ! wherefore do I see the Greeks
driven back again in confusion to the camp ?

May heaven grant that what I fear be not
come to pass, and that my brave Patroclus
be not slain.   I charged him ere he set out
to content himself with saving the ships from
being burned, and not to venture to meet
Hector in fight."

While he revolved these thoughts in his
mind, Antilochus came up with his eyes full
of tears, and said—

"Son of Peleus, I bring you evil tidings.
Patroclus has fallen, and the Greeks are
fighting hard for his naked corpse, for Hector
has stripped him of his armour."

So spoke Antilochus; and Achilles lifted up
his voice and wept aloud with an exceeding
bitter cry.   Antilochus kept fast hold of his
right hand, for he feared he might stab himself to the heart in the first agony of his grief.
At his cry, his mother Thetis came to him,
with the nymphs her sisters that bare her
company, and asked wherefore he grieved, for
the Greeks had surely suffered for the evil they
had wrought him.

"True, mother," replied Achilles, "but

what care I for that, now that my dear comrade Patroclus, whom I loved best of all my companions, has fallen? I have lost him and my armour too, which Hector has stripped from his corpse: that glorious armour which the gods gave to Peleus on his wedding day, when thou wert wedded to a mortal man. Would that he had wooed a mortal like himself! And soon shall you both grieve for me; I shall nevermore return to the halls of Peleus: for I care not to live and move among my fellow-men, till Hector falls before my spear, and atones by his death for the dishonour he has done to Patroclus."

"Alas, my child!" said Thetis, "if you slay Hector, your own life will be but brief."

Then said Achilles fiercely, "Would that I might die now, since I could not save my friend. He lies dead on a foreign shore, and I, though I never again shall see my home, yet did not help him, or any of the other Greeks whom Hector has slain. O thrice unhappy quarrel, which has forced me to sit here idle. But now will I school my

proud spirit, and go forth to war, to slay
Hector who has laid my darling low."

"In sooth, dear child," answered Thetis,
"you do well to avenge your comrade : but
the Trojans have your arms, and Hector
wears them upon his shoulders. Wait for one
day: and on the morrow I will return, and
bring you noble arms forged by Hephaestus
himself, the cunning worker in metals."

Thus saying she vanished away : but even
while she spoke the Greeks were fleeing
panic-stricken before the savage onset of
Hector : nor could they drag the corpse of
Patroclus from among the Trojans, for Hector,
terrible as a consuming fire, had laid hold of
it by the foot, and loudly urged his comrades
onward. Still, the two Ajaces doggedly
stayed by the body, and ever and anon
drove Hector back for a little space, even as
herdsmen who seek to drive a hungry lion
away from the carcase of an ox that he has
slain. Yet would Hector surely have gained
the body, had not Hêrê sent swift Iris, the
messenger of the gods, to Achilles. "Up,

son of Peleus," said she, "save thy comrade's
body ; for Hector will soon bear it off to the
breezy heights of Troy, and cast it to the
dogs."

" How can I go forth to battle ? " answered
Achilles. " The enemy have my arms. True,
I have my great ashen spear from Mount
Pelion, but nought beside it. And I know
not what other Greek's armour I could wear.
I might, indeed, make shift with the shield
of great Ajax ; but he, I trow, is using it
himself, fighting in the front rank for poor
Patroclus."

" Yet go forth," pleaded Iris, "and show
thyself ; " for sore is the need of the Greeks.
It may be that the enemy will fear thy voice
and give way."

So Achilles went forth to the outside of
the ditch. Thrice he shouted with a terrible
voice, and at his well-known battle cry the
Trojans shrank back in dread, while the
Greeks laid Patroclus upon a shield, and bore
him sadly back to the camp which he had
left so bravely in the morning. Now the

sun was setting, as Achilles, weeping bitterly, bore the body to his own tent, and there made a solemn vow that he would not bury it ere he had taken ample vengeance upon Hector.

Meanwhile the Trojans, who were far away from their city, debated whether they should return, or pass the night where they stood. Polydamas would have had them return to the shelter of the city walls, now that Achilles again fought for the Greeks; but Hector, emboldened by his victory, overruled him, and kept the host encamped upon the open plain, promising that on the morrow they should storm the camp of the Greeks.

While the Trojans rested upon the plain, Thetis had begged Hephaestus to forge new arms for her son, and already he had made a shield, stout and strong, and had wrought upon it the figure of the earth, the heavens, the sea, and all the stars that deck the skies, the Pleiads, and Orion, and the " Bear," which some call the " Wain," which circles round the pole, watching Orion, and alone of all the stars never dips beneath the waves of Ocean.

In it he wrought two cities : in the one were feastings and weddings; the bride was being led through the streets by torchlight, and loud the nuptial song arose, while youths danced to the sound of the flute, and the women looked on, each standing at the door of her house. In the market-place two men were contending about a fine, which the one declared that he had paid, and which the other said that he had never received. The heralds kept back the people, while the elders sate upon benches of polished stone, with long sceptres in their hands, hearing each man speak in turn, that they might do justice between them.

The other city was beleaguered by a host. The defenders had manned their walls with old men, women, and boys, while they went out and lay in ambush on the banks of a river. Ares and Pallas Athênê led them, wrought in gold, statelier to look upon than the rest, and of taller stature. Two spies

watched the coming of flocks of sheep and herds
of oxen, and when they drew near the men in
ambush fell upon them, while the besieging
host strove to rescue them. There, on the
river bank, they fought with brazen spears,
and amid the battle were wrought figures
of Strife, and Tumult, and deadly Fate,
dragging men by the hair through the throng
of warriors.

There too was graven a rich fallow field :
and many ploughmen drove their teams up
and down it. As they reached the end of
their furrows, a man gave each of them a
cup of sweet wine ; and they ploughed
steadfastly onward, while behind them the
ground looked black, even as a ploughed field
looks, so cunningly was it wrought.

There also he made a field standing thick
with corn ; and in it youths were reaping
with sickles in their hands. Behind them
came binders, who bound up the sheaves as
they fell, while boys carried away the sheaves
and set them up in order. Among them,
in silence, stood the king their lord, rejoicing

at the plenteous harvest, while in a corner of the field his heralds were sacrificing an ox, and women were mixing white barley porridge for the labourers' dinner.

There too was a vineyard wrought in gold : the dark heavy bunches of grapes rested on silver props. Round about it was a ditch, and a fence of shining tin. One path ran through it, for use in the vintage season, and along it walked youths and maidens, innocent and gay, bearing great baskets full of the rich ripe grapes. In the midst a boy with a lyre sang sweetly, and they moved their feet in time to the music.

There he wrought a herd of long-horned kine, with herdsmen and dogs. Two fierce lions had seized a great ox, and were tearing him to pieces with their teeth, and lapping his blood ; while the herdsmen urged on their dogs, who dared not bite the terrible lions, but stood near them barking and keeping out of reach of their paws.

There too he wrought a herd of goats in

a mountain glade; and a fair dancing-hall, wherein youths and high-born maidens were dancing, holding one another by the wrists. The maidens were clad in dainty robes of white, and the youths in woven tunics : the maidens were crowned with flowers, while the youths wore golden swords and silver belts.   There they turned and wheeled in the dance, while round them stood a crowd, admiring, and a minstrel sang to the music of the lyre, and two tumblers showed their tricks.

Round about the shield, on the outermost rim, he wrought the mighty stream of Ocean, that flows round all the world.

When Hephaestus had finished the shield, he wrought a corslet that shone like the sun at noon, and a helmet of cunning workman-ship, with a golden plume, and light greaves of shining tin.

When he had finished the work, he laid it all before silver-footed Thetis ; and she and her nymphs swiftly bore it away.

HOW ACHILLES SLEW HECTOR

K

CHAPTER VIII

How Achilles slew Hector

ALL night long Achilles mourned over the body of Patroclus. At break of day Thetis came with her nymphs, bringing the arms. Terribly did they flash in the beams of the rising sun, and the Myrmidons shrank affrighted at the sight, but Achilles sternly rejoiced, for the arms reminded him of the task before him, to avenge his comrade. While Thetis watched beside the body of Patroclus, anointing it with ambrosia lest it should decay, Achilles strode along the seashore, calling aloud to all the Greeks to assemble together. At his voice all came gladly, Odysseus and Diomedes with limping gait, for they were still crippled by their wounds, and Agamemnon came last of all, for he was ill at ease from the hurt which Koon, the son of Antenor, had dealt him. Then Achilles said—

"Agamemnon, it is not right for us two to be at variance any longer. Would that Briseis, the cause of our quarrel, had never lived: that would have saved the life of many a brave Greek who has fallen while I have been withdrawn in my anger. But now let us forgive what is past, and lay aside our pride. I am willing to forgive all that you have done, only let us as quickly as may be arm the Greeks for battle. Happy will be the Trojan who this day escapes my spear."

Agamemnon answered—

"Heroes and friends, hear, all of ye, my words. I was distraught, and not in my right mind, what time I insulted Achilles. Often have I sorrowed for my fault, and grievously have I atoned for it. But now I would fain become his friend, and will send costly presents, and Briseis herself, unharmed and pure as when she came to me, either to your tent, Achilles, or to you here if you will remain with me. After that we will make ready for battle."

Achilles answered, "Agamemnon, I am your friend, and I thank you for your presents. But we have much to do before Achilles can again be seen leading the van, scattering the Trojans with his spear. Let every man arm himself for the fight, and do as I do."

At this, however, Odysseus interfered, warning Achilles not to lead the Greeks fasting to battle; and while they were making ready their breakfast, Briseis was brought to the tent of Achilles. When she saw Patroclus lying there dead, she fell upon the body and kissed it, weeping over it, for Patroclus had ever been gentle and good to her. With her wept her maidens, in outward show, for Patroclus, but each in her heart wept over her own sorrows.

Achilles, too, felt a keen pang when he remembered how often he and Patroclus had shared their morning meal together, and these thoughts made him eager to lead the

Greeks out of the camp, and begin the fray.

When Achilles attacked the Trojans, the old songs say that the Immortals themselves came down from Olympus to take part in the battle. First Apollo, in the likeness of Lycaon, one of the sons of Priam, urged Æneas to withstand Achilles. Æneas met him face to face, and hurled his spear, but he could not pierce the splendid shield of Achilles, and Achilles in turn struck through the shield of Æneas, but missed his body. Æneas hurled a great stone at Achilles before he could recover his spear ; yet had not Aphrodite snatched him away betimes, Æneas would surely have fallen. Onward pressed Achilles, slaughtering all whom he met. He slew Polydorus, a son of Priam, and for a moment Hector came forward to fight over his brother's body, but his hour was not yet come, and the two warriors were parted, while Achilles raged like a fire in a dry copse upon a mountain side, that scorches up every living thing that comes in its path. Fast fled the Trojans before him,

till they reached the banks of eddying Xanthus,
where some of them escaped from him, while
others plunged into the waters and were swept
away.   Here Achilles, among many others,
slew Lycaon, though he begged for mercy ;
but Achilles sternly answered that Patroclus
was dead, though a better man than he, and
that he too must die.   So down the stream
into the sea floated the corpse of Lycaon,
while Achilles assailed the brave Paeonian,
Asteropaeus, who fought with a spear in each
hand, and hurled them both together at
Achilles.   One struck his shield, but could
not pierce it : but the other grazed his
forearm, and the blood gushed forth.   Then
Achilles hurled his spear with mighty force,
but it missed Asteropaeus, and struck the
lofty river bank behind him, where ·it remained quivering, fixed in the cliff to half its
length.   Achilles now drew his sword and
rushed upon Asteropaeus, who thrice vainly
tugged at the spear, hoping to draw it out
and use it in his own defence.   He then
tried to break it off: but ere he could do so,

Achilles laid him dead at his feet. Drawing out his spear from the cliff, Achilles fell upon the Paeonians till the river was choked with their dead.

Upon a lofty tower stood old King Priam, until he saw the Trojans give way before Achilles. Then he bade the warders fling the city gates open wide, that the flying host might pour in. Parched with thirst and begrimed with mire the breathless Trojans made for the city, while Achilles, spear in hand, pressed on the hindmost. Then surely he might have taken the city, had not a moment's breathing space been gained by bold Agenor, Antenor's son, who checked Achilles, and struck him on the knee. Yet Achilles was not wounded, nor would Agenor have escaped had not Phoebus Apollo in his likeness beguiled Achilles, and led him away upon a fruitless chase.

Meanwhile the Trojans poured fast into the city: yet Hector still remained without. In vain did Priam beseech him to save himself, and enter the gate, for the old man saw

the bright arms of Achilles shining afar off,
with a baleful light, and knew that Achilles
was drawing nearer and nearer. With both
hands stretched out over the city walls Priam
called to him, " Hector, my best beloved son,
await not the charge of Achilles alone, lest
you die. Terrible is he in battle, and many
of my children has he slain. Indeed, this
day, I cannot see my two sons, Lycaon and
Polydorus, returning from battle, and I fear
that they both must have fallen. Yet, grieved
though I and their mother would be at their
loss, it will be as nothing compared with your
death. Enter the gate : have pity on me,
miserable old man that I am, doomed to see
my sons struck down, my daughters led away
captive, my city taken, and myself to be slain
and cast to the dogs."

So spoke Priam ; and Hecuba, by his side,
with tears pointed to her breast, at which
Hector had been nursed, imploring him to
come in ; yet Hector, leaning his shield
against the basement of the city wall, stood
firm, awaiting the coming of Achilles, even

as a snake upon a mountain side, which, charged with deadly venom, awaits a traveller, hissing as it coils around its lair, while its eyes gleam red with hate and rage. And thus he communed with himself :

"Woe is me : if I enter the city, Polydamas will be the first to reproach me with having brought destruction upon my countrymen on that fatal night when Achilles came forth, and I withstood his better counsel. But now, since by my folly I have caused such ruin, I well might blush to meet the men of Troy, and the Trojan ladies with their trailing robes, lest some of them should say, 'Hector in his blind conceit brought ruin upon the people.' Better stay here and die, if I may not slay Achilles and return in triumph. Vain would it be to beg for mercy : I must fight or fall."

While Hector mused thus, Achilles, terrible as Ares, his golden armour flashing in the sun, came fiercely onward, brandishing aloft his great ashen spear. At the sight Hector's heart failed him, and he ran. Achilles rushed after him, and swiftly they raced round and

round the walls of Troy, past the watch-tower,
beneath the wall near the fig-tree, and along
the high-road that leads to the hot and cold
fountains and the washing-troughs of polished
stone, where, in the happy peaceful days of
old, before the Greeks came to the land, the
wives and daughters of the Trojans were
wont to wash their clothes. Thrice they
raced round Troy : Father Zeus sorrowed
for Hector, and would fain have saved him,
but Pallas Athênê called upon him not to
interpose to save a mortal man. Then, as
they circled round the city for the fourth
time, Zeus raised aloft the golden scales of
Fate, and placed in each a lot, one for Hector,
and one for swift-footed Achilles. Down
sank the scale of Hector, weighted with his
death, down to the shades below, and Phoebus
Apollo left his side. Now Pallas, in the
likeness of Deiphobus, came to Hector, and
bade him stand firm, and they two would do
their best to face Achilles. Hector stayed,
and challenged Achilles to fight. Achilles
hurled his spear, but missed his mark. Then

Hector threw his own spear, but it glanced aside from the shield of Achilles, and Hector loudly called upon Deiphobus to give him a second spear. But no Deiphobus was there. Hector saw that he had been fooled, and, drawing his sword, dashed forward against Achilles, who, by the help of Pallas, had regained his spear, and now, watching his chance, struck Hector where the collar-bone parts the neck from the shoulder. Down fell Hector in the dust, and Achilles savagely taunted him that he had not long enjoyed his victory over Patroclus. Hector, though breath was failing him, begged that his body might be given to his friends for burial, but Achilles sternly answered, " Talk not to me of ransom, nor of burial. Nought can save you from being cast to the dogs,—no, not any ransom that you can name. Never shall thy mother weep over thy corpse, but carrion vultures shall tear it."

Then answered Hector faintly, for the hand of death was upon him, " I cannot hope to change your iron purpose. Yet fear

the wrath of Heaven, when by the Scaean
gate Paris shall strike you down, for all you
be so brave a warrior."

So speaking he died : and though he was
dead, Achilles answered him, "Die! when
Heaven wills it I will meet my fate."

As he spoke, he stripped the body of its
armour, and for a moment thought that he
would essay to take the city of Troy : but
when he bethought him that his dear Patroclus
lay yet unburied, he bade the Greeks return
to their camp, and they went back, singing
glad paeans of joy at their victory.   Achilles
himself tied Hector's feet to his chariot,
using the same sword-belt which Ajax had
given to Hector after their fight, and dragged
the body on the ground as he drove along.
At the sight of Hector's fair hair trailing in
the dust his mother shrieked aloud and tore
her gray locks, while Priam would fain have
gone forth to beg for the body of his noblest
son.   Nor was aught as yet known to
Hector's wife Andromache : she sate weaving
at her loom, and bade her maidens warm a

bath against her lord's return from the
battle: but he already lay dead upon the
plain. Then as she heard weeping and
wailing in the streets without, she started up,
and cried—

"Follow me, my maids : my mind mis-
gives me that some evil is at hand. I hear
my mother's voice; my heart beats fast; my
limbs refuse to move. Some evil hath
chanced. O pray that it be not so; that
Hector's courage hath not led him to fight
Achilles alone, and to fall."

So speaking she rushed in frenzy out of
the house, and when she mounted on the
wall, saw Hector's body trailing in the dust
as Achilles swiftly drove his chariot away.
Darkness came over poor Andromache's
eyes at that dreadful sight, and she fainted
away in the arms of Cassandra, her husband's
sister. When she came to herself she piteously made her moan over him.

"Hector, we both were born to misery,—I
in woody Thebe, and thou here in Troy.
Now thou art gone, leaving bitterest grief to

me and to thy child. Thou never canst defend him now, nor can he ever be a help to
thee. Even should he be spared in this dreadful war, yet strangers will take his heritage,
and none will protect the orphan boy. He
must stand, in tears, pinched with hunger,
and pluck his father's old comrades by the
cloak as they sit at table, if perchance one of
them will give him a morsel of food. Then
youths whose fathers are alive will bid him
begone, and he will flee for refuge to his
widowed mother's arms, he, that Astyanax, who
erst was fed with dainties on his father's knees,
and was lulled to sleep upon his nurse's bosom."

Thus spoke she weeping, and all her
maidens lamented with her.

Now Achilles buried Patroclus splendidly,
and held games at his tomb, as was the custom
in those times. First there was a chariot-race,
which was won by Diomedes, with the swift
horses which he had taken from Æneas ; and
Antilochus, Nestor's son, came in second, for
old Nestor had told him how to drive. But
Menelaus was not satisfied, and declared

that Antilochus had got in his way, and had
not raced fairly. Then Antilochus took the
horse which was to have been his prize, and
offered it to Menelaus, saying that he never
would dispute with an older man than himself; so Menelaus was appeased, and gave
him back his horse. And Achilles gave
Nestor a silver bowl: for he loved and
revered the good old man. Next there was
a boxing match, which was won by Epeus,
and a wrestling match between Odysseus and
Telamonian Ajax, in which it was hard to
say which was the best man. Neither could
throw the other: and at last Ajax said,
" Odysseus, lift me off my feet, if you can,
or let me lift you, and let us see what will
befall." So saying, he lifted up Odysseus;
but Odysseus cunningly struck Ajax behind
the knee with his foot, and threw him backwards. Next Odysseus lifted Ajax, though
he could only just raise his great weight from
the ground : yet he crooked his knee so that
they both fell together, and then Achilles
bade them cease, and gave them each a prize.

A foot-race was won by Odysseus, for Ajax the son of Öileus stumbled and fell close to the winning post. Young Antilochus was third, and said that it seemed vain to strive with older men, for Ajax was a little older than himself, while Odysseus was quite an elderly man, and yet could run faster than any of the Greeks save only swift-footed Achilles himself.

Next Achilles brought forth a spear, a helmet, and a shield, the arms of Sarpedon, which Patroclus had stripped from his dead body, and bade two heroes fight in armour for them, promising to the vanquished a fine Thracian sword, which he himself had taken from Asteropaeus. Then Ajax the son of Telamon, and Diomedes the son of Tydeus fought fiercely, till all the heroes feared that they would slay one another ; and they parted the spoils between them.

In throwing a huge mass of iron Poly-poetes was the winner, for he threw it far beyond Ajax, Epeus, or Leontes; and in

L

archery Meriones beat Teucer, and won ten axes.

In hurling the spear Agamemnon far surpassed every one, and won a cauldron of bright brass, while Meriones was given a long spear.

HOW THE GREEKS FOUGHT
THE AMAZONS

CHAPTER IX

How the Greeks fought the Amazons

WHEN the games were over the heroes went home to their suppers and their beds; but Achilles could neither eat nor sleep, but mourned all night long for his dear companion. On the morrow he again tied Hector's body to his chariot, and dragged it round the tomb of Patroclus; and thus he did day after day, until Father Zeus became displeased with him, and sent his mother Thetis to persuade him to give back the body, and to put away his wrath. Meanwhile Zeus sent a thought into the mind of old King Priam, as he lay in his palace grieving for Hector; and when evening was come, Priam chose the richest robes from his treasure-chests for presents, bade his sons, Paris, Helenus, Deiphobus, and the rest, harness his horses to a chariot, and mules to a waggon, placed the presents in the waggon, and made ready to set out for the camp of the Greeks, with only old Idaeus the herald. When Hecuba his queen saw him making ready to go, she wept aloud and said, " Ah me, where is now the wisdom for which once you were famed? How can you think of going to the camp of the foe, and into the presence of that savage warrior who hath slain our Hector, and so many of our children besides. He will show no mercy when once he catches sight of you. I hate him: for he slew our noble son when he was fighting bravely in defence of Troy. Go not unto him, but let us nurse our grief here in silence."

Priam answered her, " Wife, seek not to hinder me, for I am resolved to go, and nought that you can say will hold me back. If it be my fate, let Achilles slay me beside his black ships. I am content to die, if only

once again I may hold my boy in my arms,
and give my sorrow vent.   Besides, I think
that the gods themselves wish me to go, and
that they will watch over me."

So saying he called to his sons, and they
brought the chariot and the waggon.   Hecuba
brought a goblet of wine, and Priam and
Idaeus, after they had drunk and poured a
libation to the gods, set forth through the
night.   When they were come to the ford of
the river Xanthus, and the horses and mules
were drinking, they saw a figure moving
towards them.   Then said Idaeus, " Here
comes some foeman : let us quickly settle
what we must do, whether it were better
to flee in the chariot and let him take the
waggon, or to fall at his feet and beseech him
not to harm us."   Thus he spoke, and old
Priam was sore afraid, but the stranger greeted
him courteously, and asked him whither he
was driving through the night.   Then, when
the two old men had regained their courage,
the stranger said that he guessed who Priam
was, and upon what errand he was bound,

and added, that he himself was one of the Myrmidons, and would lead him safely to Achilles. So they drove forward, with the stranger for their guide. When they were come to the door of Achilles's tent, the stranger said, "Hector lies within; his body is uncorrupted, for the gods have watched over him. Go in, and fear not; but entreat Achilles to give him up to you, and to accept the ransom which you bring. And know that I am Hermes, and that Father Zeus hath sent me to guide you hither in safety."

So Priam passed in alone. Achilles had just supped, and the table still stood beside him, though Automedon and Alcimus, his brave comrades, had removed the meat. Priam avoided them, came up to Achilles, and taking him by the hand fell on his knees before him, kissing his terrible murderous hands, which had slain so many of his sons. Achilles was astonished, and so were all who stood by, but Priam besought him, saying—

"Think, great Achilles, of your own father. He, like me, is now feeble and old: and he

too, perchance, is wronged by his neighbours,
and hath none to help him. Yet he knows
that his son lives, and hopes one day to see
him return : but I, poor wretch, have lost
my best beloved son Hector, whom you slew
fighting for his country. For his dear sake
I have dared to come to the ships of the
Greeks, and now, I pray you, Achilles,
reverence the gods, and pity me; for sure
never man on earth hath borne such grief as I,
who stoop to kiss the hands that slew my son."

As Priam spoke, a fond memory of his
father rose within the breast of Achilles. He
raised the old man gently from the ground,
and they both wept. Priam wept for Hector,
and Achilles for Patroclus, and for his pleasant
home in Phthia, far beyond the sea. At last
Achilles spoke :

"Old man, how dared you come hither
into the midst of your foes, to me, who have
slain your sons? surely yours is an iron
heart. But now sit down, and let us cease
from weeping, grieved though we be : for
thus doth Zeus mingle good and evil in the

lives of mortal men. He gave to Peleus wealth and strength, and an Immortal for his bride, and made him king over the Myrmidons; but he gave him no son to succeed him in his kingdom save me : and I shall never gladden his old age, for here I must remain before Troy, working evil to thee and to thy children until I die. You too, I am told, were once a great king, ruling all the land from holy Lesbos to the Hellespont; but now your kingdom is lost, and your city like to fall. Wherefore weep not; for tears will not bring your Hector back to life."

Thus spoke Achilles, and bade Automedon and Alcimus bring the body of Hector, and place it in the waggon, from which they took the presents, leaving two of the robes to cover the body. Then Achilles killed a sheep, and his comrades skinned and divided it into joints, which they roasted over the clear embers of the wood fire. When it was cooked, Achilles said courteously to Priam :

" Eat, old man, for you are my guest. The

body of Hector is yours, and with the morning light you may take it home with you to
Troy.   But now eat, grieved though you be;
for even Niobe ate food, though Phoebus
Apollo slew all her children with his arrows.
Nine days she grieved for them, but on the
tenth day the Immortals buried them, and
she arose and ate meat."

So saying, Achilles took Priam by the
hand, and led him to the table.   Automedon
placed bread beside them in a fair basket,
and Achilles carved the meat.   When they
had eaten and drunk, they sat on opposite
sides of the tent, looking at one another.
Priam could not but admire Achilles as he
sate full of youth and strength, like one of
the Immortals come down from Olympus;
while Achilles admired Priam, for he was a
stately old man, with a noble presence, and
he spoke as becomes a king.

Achilles had bidden his servants make
beds for Priam and old Idaeus, in a part of
his tent where no one would see them, if
perchance any of the chiefs should come to

take counsel with him during the night.
And there they slept; but ere the day
dawned, Hermes, sent by Father Zeus,
roused Priam, and guided him safely through
the Greek camp with Hector's body, as far
as the gates of Troy. There he vanished
away, and all the Trojans poured forth to
meet Hector's body, summoned by Cassandra,
who had watched for her father's return from
the highest tower of Troy. Hector's wife
and mother were the first to embrace his
body, and when it was carried into the
palace, Andromache wept over it, saying—

"Thou art gone, then, leaving me desolate:
nor dare I hope that I shall see my son grow
up to man's estate, for Troy will soon fall
now that thy arm no longer guards it. I
shall be borne away a captive beyond the
sea, and with me my child, to labour as a
slave, unless some Greek, whose brother or
whose kinsman Hector slew, avenge his fall
by killing the poor babe. Bitterly doth all
the city mourn for thee, Hector; but my grief
is the keenest of all, that I was not there to

close thy eyes, to clasp thy dying hand, and to treasure up thy last words in my heart."

So she spoke, and all the women wept with her.

Then Hecuba said, "Hector, dearest to me of all my children, surely when you were alive the Immortals loved you well. Even now in death they are not unmindful of you, for though many of my sons have been slain far away, or sent captive beyond the sea, yet fierce Achilles hath sent you back to me, and there you lie as beautiful as erst in life."

She ceased, and beauteous Helen spoke in turn :

"Hector, of all my brothers-in-law, you were the dearest to me. I have now dwelt long in Troy, the bride of Paris; would I had perished ere I came : but never have I heard from you one scornful or unkind word. Nay, if any one reproached me, either your sisters, your brothers, or their wives, or Hecuba herself, for Priam always was good to me, you always checked them and pro-tected me with tender feeling and gentle words. I weep for you, and no less for myself: for in all wide Troy no one is left who loves me now. I have no friend: all shrink from me as from one accursed."

While the women mourned thus, Priam bade the people go forth to Mount Ida and fetch wood for Hector's funeral pile. Achilles had promised that he would not let the Greeks attack them before Hector was buried: and they made a splendid funeral pile, and burned his body upon it. When Hector was buried, the Trojans no longer ventured outside the city walls, for fear of Achilles; and they began to fear that the Greeks would surely take Troy. But soon they regained their courage: for from the banks of the river Thermodon came Penthesilea, the brave and beautiful queen of the Amazons. She had by mischance slain her sister, Hippolyte, with a javelin while hunting, and as after this she could not bear to remain at home, she came to Troy to fight for her old friend and ally, King Priam. With her came twelve other Amazons, her

comrades, tall and strong, and well skilled
in war ; and in the midst of them rode
Penthesilea in the pride of her beauty, even
as the full moon shines in the midst of the
stars in the calm clear summer sky.   Her
presence was welcome to the Trojans as rain
to a thirsty land ; and when they looked
upon her, they felt that, with such a leader,
they might still hope for victory.   Even
Priam rejoiced when he saw her, broken-
hearted though he was at the death of his
children.   He bade her welcome to Troy,
and led her into his own palace, as kindly
as though she were his own daughter, come
home again after long wandering in foreign
lands.   That night he feasted her royally,
and gave her splendid gifts, promising her
much more if she would save Troy from the
Greeks.   Penthesilea, on her part, was not
backward, but loudly boasted that she would
overthrow the Grecian host, and Achilles
himself, and would burn their ships.   Little
knew she of the strength of Achilles, and his
power in battle.

When Andromache heard her speak thus, she softly murmured to herself, " Poor fool, why talk thus wildly ? You have not strength to meet Achilles in fight : in sooth, your death is nigh. Hector was a far better warrior than you can be, and yet Achilles slew him, while all Troy looked on and wept, and since that day I have never ceased to grieve."

Thus thought Eetion's fair daughter, as she looked upon Penthesilea ; but aloud she said not a word.

After the banquet, Penthesilea slept in King Priam's palace ; and at break of day she gaily arose and put on her shining arms. Her shield was shaped like a half-moon, and the crest of her helmet sparkled with gold. In her left hand she bore two javelins, and in her right a mighty battle-axe. Mounted on a noble steed, with her Amazons around her, she proudly led forth the Trojans to a battle whence many of them were doomed never to return, while Priam prayed aloud to Father Zeus : but he turned his face away from Troy.

The Greeks were taken by surprise: for
they knew not of Penthesilea's coming, and
did not expect to see the Trojans sally forth
so boldly. At first it seemed as though
Penthesilea would make good her boast, for
she struck down man after man, while one
of her comrades slew Menippus, a friend of
Protesilaus. Podarkes struck the Amazon
dead; but Penthesilea avenged her comrade's
fall, and drove a spear through the body of
Podarkes. Idomeneus and Meriones now
came up, and Ajax, the son of Öileus, who
bravely withstood the charge of the Amazons,
and slew several of them. But Penthesilea
exultingly dashed into the midst of the Greeks,
followed by Hector's brothers, and all the
bravest of the Trojans. Dire was the havoc
that she wrought, and the Trojans began to
hope that the day would be theirs; for
Achilles and great Ajax had been sitting
mourning beside the tomb of Patroclus, and
had not hitherto had time to reach the battle.
When these two redoubted heroes were come,
they dealt destruction among the Amazons,

M

but Penthesilea eagerly galloped towards them, to try her strength with the bravest of the Greeks. She hurled one of her darts at Achilles, but could not pierce his famous shield, and with the other she struck Ajax on the greaves, yet did not wound him.

Ajax took no heed of Penthesilea, but turned to attack another of her band, leaving her alone with Achilles, who stepped forward and drove his great ashen spear through her breastplate and into her breast. Sightless and dizzy, Penthesilea reeled beneath that fearful stroke, and her axe fell from her hand. Yet she was not mortally hurt, and as she dimly saw Achilles advancing, she hesitated, wondering whether it would be best for her to draw her sword from its sheath, and try to keep him off, or to dismount from her horse, and beg for mercy. While she mused thus, Achilles fiercely hurled his great spear, and pierced both Penthesilea and the horse on which she rode, that they fell together to the ground, quivering in the

death-agony. Her long fair tresses mingled
with the horse's mane as she lay, lovely as
Artemis resting from the chase, while around
her the affrighted Trojans urged their steeds
to flight, and far away the walls of Troy
gleamed white in the noonday sunshine.
Achilles, when he had drawn out his spear
from Penthesilea's dead body, and kneeled
down to take off her helmet, was touched by
the sight of her beauty; and tears rose to his
eyes when he thought how far better it had
been for him to have taken the noble lady to
his pleasant home in Phthia, and to have
dwelt happily there in peace, with her for his
bride, instead of wasting all his days in
useless strife and bloodshed. As he stood
gazing upon her, his brow overshadowed by
these remorseful thoughts, the wretched Thersites, who was standing hard by, jeered at
him, saying, " Achilles, why grieve you over
that hateful Amazon ? She would fain have
done mischief to you and to me : and now
you must needs sorrow for her as though she
had been your promised bride. Would that

she had struck you with her spear, since you care nought for glory and honour, in your lust for her fair face. Remember what trouble has come upon the Trojans because they hankered after strange women, even as you do now."

Thus spoke Thersites, and his words stirred Achilles to anger. He struck Thersites with his fist upon the mouth, that all his teeth were dashed out, and he fell dead, with blood streaming from his mouth. All the Greeks rejoiced when they saw Thersites fall, and they muttered one to another, "It is an ill thing to insult a king. A ribald tongue brings ruin on its owner, and that with justice, for it causes more mischief than aught else on earth."

Diomedes alone of the Greeks was angry with Achilles for having slain Thersites, who was his kinsman. He and Achilles would have come to blows, had not the other chiefs held them back. And then, full of pity and admiration for the noble Penthesilea, they reverently raised her body from the ground,

and sent it back to Troy for burial. But
Achilles, after he had slain Thersites, went
away to Lesbos, and there the priests puri-
fied him from blood-guiltiness, and sent him
back in peace.

HOW PARIS SLEW ACHILLES

CHAPTER X

How Paris slew Achilles

THE Trojans now held a council to
settle what should be done. Old
Thymoetes said:

" We can fight no longer, now that Hector
has fallen. I fear me that Achilles will make
his way over our walls, and burn and slay,
for none of us can withstand his might. See
how he slew the great Penthesilea, glorious
warrior though she was. I myself thought
when I saw her that one of the Immortals
had come down from Olympus to help us, so
strong and so fair was she; yet he laid her
low. Can we indeed hold out any longer,
or has the hour come for us to flee away, and
yield up our fair city to the Greeks?"

Then answered King Priam, "Thymoetes, let us not leave our city, but let us
stay within the shelter of its walls at least
until Memnon comes; and I have good hope
that he will soon be here. Let us endure
yet a little longer, hard pressed though we
be. Whatever may befall, it is better for us
to die like men, with our faces to the foe,
than to flee away and dwell in exile de-
pendent on strangers."

Thus spoke Priam: but the wise Polydamas,
who was weary of the war, answered him :

" If the noble Memnon is indeed nigh at
hand, I trust that he may save our city and
ourselves; yet I sadly fear that he too may
fall, for who can withstand the might of
Achilles and the Greeks ? But come, let us
neither disgrace ourselves by fleeing from
our city, nor yet remain in it to be
slaughtered, but let us, late though it be,
give up lovely Helen and the treasure which
she brought hither from Sparta, and · more
besides, twice or thrice as much if need be,
to save our homes from the spoiler and our

city from the flames. Thus let us do, for
no better counsel can be given."

Thus spoke wise Polydamas : and all the
Trojan chiefs felt that he was right, yet
none liked to let his thoughts be seen.
Paris harshly reproached him, saying :

" Polydamas, you shun the battlefield. A
coward in fight, you would fain be thought
prudent in the council, but your advice is
foolishness. Stay at home if you wish it,
but meanwhile the rest of the hardy Trojans
will follow me to the field, for men win
honour in battle, and only women, and woman-
ish men like you, skulk behind, and damp
the spirit of the rest."

Angrily did Polydamas reply:

" Most hateful of men, your daring has
brought sorrow and suffering upon us all, and
your counsel will ruin our city. May I never
dare such deeds as thine, but keep my head
cool, and my home safe."

So spoke Polydamas, and Paris dared not
reply, for he knew that he was the cause of the
war, and he would have died rather than give

up fair Helen, for whose sake the Trojans
were keeping watch on their walls under
arms, lest the Greeks should assault the town.

Soon after this the noble Memnon came,
with a countless host of dusky warriors from
Æthiopia. The Trojan princes flocked
round him, bidding him welcome to Troy,
and Priam was glad at heart when he marked
the strength and gallant bearing of his guest,
and his splendid arms. Memnon had much
to tell of his long journey, and of the fierce
Solymi, who had fought with him on the
way, so that he had not been able to reach
Troy earlier, while Priam told him of all
that had come to pass since the landing of
the Greeks. At the banquet Priam pledged
Memnon in an ancient golden cup of curious
workmanship, which Hephaestus himself had
wrought for one of Priam's forefathers.
Priam now gave the cup to Memnon, and
bade him drink to the success of his arms on
the morrow. Memnon thanked him, and
modestly said that he must not boast while
there was no danger, but he hoped that

Priam would soon see that he was no coward.

On the next day Memnon led forth his host in company with the Trojans, and a great and terrible battle was fought. The two armies fell upon one another even as the angry billows of the sea, when a strong west wind blows, and the solid earth trembled beneath the trampling of their feet and the shouts of defiance on either side. Far to the right, Achilles slew two noble Trojans, Thalius and Mentes, and many a warrior besides, for he raged in the fight like a fierce whirlwind that uproots tall trees and casts down walls and houses in ruin ; while, on the other wing, Memnon pressed hard upon the men of Elis and sandy Pylos. He struck down Pheron and Ereuthon, who dwelt in Thryon beside the stream of Alpheus, and had followed old Nestor, their chief, to Troy. When Memnon had stripped them of their arms, he aimed his spear at Nestor himself, and would have slain him had not young Antilochus sprung before his sire, and hurled

his spear at Memnon, just missing him, but
striking down his comrade, Pyrrhasides the
Æthiop, who stood by his side. Enraged at
the death of his friend, Memnon sprang to
attack Antilochus, who bravely stood his
ground, and struck Memnon on the helmet
with a great stone, but Memnon drove his
spear through the corslet of Antilochus into
his heart, and he fell dead. At his fall his
father Nestor grieved sore, and loudly called
Thrasymedes and Phereus to his aid. Yet
they could not stand before the great king of
Æthiopia, and old Nestor himself rushed
forward and would surely have lost his life,
had not Memnon recognised him, and courteously warned him to fall back, saying that
he never would lift his hand against one who
had known his own father, but that he had
taken Nestor to be some young warrior by
his fighting so bravely in the front rank.
So Nestor, grieved to the heart, went away in
search of Achilles, and begged him to fight with
Memnon, and avenge the fall of Antilochus.

When Achilles met Memnon, all around

paused, awestricken ; so terrible was the fight between the two heroes. They drew their swords, and stood face to face, arrayed in their gleaming armour, their broad shoulders towering above the throng of warriors in the majesty of their strength. Each keenly watched the other, looking over the rims of their shields, while ever and anon their lofty plumes seemed to mingle as they struck fiercely at one another : for each fought with fury, and recked not that his fate was nigh. Blood was flowing from many a wound, and sweat poured down their mighty limbs as they battled on unweariedly, while the light dust rose with the trampling of their feet and hung in a cloud overhead. All the Immortals watched the strife, for each was dear to them, and each was goddess-born. At last Zeus lifted high the scales of Fate. Down sank the scale of Memnon, weighted with his death, and Achilles struck him through the breast, while Eos his mother shrieked, and covered all the plain with darkness, while she snatched away the body of her beloved child, and buried it beside the Hellespont, near the banks of dark Æsepus. And there from his ashes sprang black-plumaged birds, which come every year to his tomb and fight one another there to this day.

As soon as they saw Memnon fall, the Trojans and Æthiopians turned and fled. Rejoicing at his victory, Achilles pursued, hoping that now at last Troy might be won : but as he pressed the flying host toward the Scaean gate, Paris shot him dead with an arrow.

When Achilles fell, the Trojans rallied, and would have seized his body, but great Ajax stoutly bestrode it, holding his huge shield between it and the foe, while Odysseus fought bravely by his side. When Glaucus, at the head of his Lycians, charged forward towards the body, Ajax struck him dead with his spear, and during the panic and confusion made by his fall, Odysseus, covered by Ajax with his great shield, took up Achilles on his broad shoulders, arms and all, and bore him out of the fray.

The Greeks grieved over Achilles more
bitterly than over any of the other heroes
who had fallen before Troy. The whole
army built him a splendid funeral pile, and
fair Thetis herself came to the camp of the
Myrmidons to mourn for her gallant son, cut
off in the flower of his youth, even as the
oracle had ᴠforetold. With her came the
Nereids her sisters, and many more of the
Immortals, for Achilles was dear to all of
them. After Thetis and Briseis had wept
over his body, the Myrmidons burned it
upon the funeral pile, flinging their choicest
treasures into the flames the while, to show
honour to their king. As the fire sank
down, they quenched its ashes with wine,
gathered together his bones, and buried them
at the point of Cape Sigeum, hard by the
sparkling waters of the Hellespont. There
they piled a great mound over him, which
Alexander the Great saw when he landed
there on his way to India, and travellers tell
us that it stands there to this day.

After the burial of Achilles, Thetis called

N

together the chiefs of the Greeks, and told them that she herself would hold funeral games in honour of her son. Then Nestor rose, grieved though he was for his son Antilochus, and with his harp sang the praise of the noble Nereid Thetis, and how she surpassed all her sisters in beauty and wisdom. Then he sang of Peleus, how he caught her in the cave by the sea, and made her his bride, and how the Immortals feasted at his wedding, when Hebe and the Hours waited at the table, pouring nectar for the guests, and Hephaestus made a clear fire, and the Muses sang while the Graces danced, and the guests rejoiced together till all the crags of Pelion rang again, and old Cheiron's cave echoed with their mirth. Then he sang of Achilles, the child of Thetis, and praised him for his strength and manhood, telling of his fight with Cycnus and Troilus, and how he took Lyrnessus and Thebe under Placos, and how he fought the Trojans, and made their river run red with blood, until he slew brave Hector. Then he told how Achilles over-

threw Penthesilea and Memnon, and how
mighty he was in battle, so that none could
stand before him, and how swiftly he could
run races on foot, and how he was the bravest
and most beautiful of all who came against
Troy.   And all the heroes shouted aloud and
clapped their hands at Nestor's song.

Thetis rewarded old Nestor with a pair of
swift horses, which Telephus gave to Achilles
for healing his wound, long ago : and next
Teucer and Ajax the son of Öileus started to
run a race for some oxen which Achilles had
driven away from Mount Ida, albeit Æneas
had striven to save them.   Teucer would
have won the race, but that just at the end
of it he stumbled and sprained his ankle.
Machaon and Podalirius bound up Teucer's
ankle, while Ajax drove off the oxen in
triumph.

Next great Ajax and Diomedes wrestled.
Long they struggled equally, stamping till
the ground was beaten hard beneath their
feet, and the sweat poured from their limbs,
until at last Ajax seized the son of Tydeus

round the waist, hoping to throw him ; but Diomedes cleverly slipped on one side, got his shoulder under the thick of Ajax's thigh, and then, crooking his leg round Ajax's other knee, brought him headlong to the ground.

Ajax leaped to his feet and closed again with Diomedes, and they swayed backwards and forwards, clutching one another firmly, while all the host shouted, some encouraging Ajax, and some Diomedes. Then Ajax shook Diomedes by the shoulders, and while he was unsteady, slipped down his hands, and flung him backwards. They would have tried a third fall, but Nestor bade them cease and divide the prize between them.

The next prize was for boxing ; but when old Idomeneus rose, no one dared to meet him, for he was strong and wary, and well skilled in all the games which heroes love. So Thetis gave him the prize—the horses and chariot of Sarpedon, which Patroclus took from the Trojans, what time he slew Sarpedon beside the ships of the Greeks.

Then Nestor said, that though the younger

men might fear to meet Idomeneus, yet that
two of them might well box with one another.
Hereupon rose Epeus, the son of Panopeus,
who helped to slay the great wild boar, and
Acamas, the son of Theseus and Phaedra.
They bound the tough bull's hide round
their hands, and stood facing each other,
like two fierce lions who fight in a mountain
glade over the carcase of a deer.   Each shook
his arms aloft, to try whether much fighting
with spear and shield had made them stiff and
out of practice at boxing, and then they began
to spar with one another.   Epeus pressed
Acamas, but Acamas struck between Epeus's
hands, and cut his eyebrow to the bone: yet
as he did so Epeus struck him on the temple,
and rolled him on the ground.   Acamas
started up, and again assailed Epeus, striking
him on the head ; but as Acamas fell back,
Epeus struck him on the forehead with his
left hand, and on the nose with his right.
When Acamas would have attacked him
again, the Greeks parted them, and Thetis
gave them each a silver cup.

Teucer, in spite of his sprain, beat Ajax the Locrian, in archery, for he shore the plume off a helmet with an arrow, and won the armour of Troilus, which fair Thetis gave him for his prize.

Great Ajax flung an iron weight farther than any other hero, and Thetis gave him the glittering armour of Memnon, which well fitted his tall stature, weeping the while, for Ajax was strong and fair, and reminded her of her lost Achilles.

The chariot-race was won by Menelaus; for Thoas and Eurypylus drove too near one another and upset. While the physicians were tending their bruises, Thetis gave Menelaus an embossed silver cup, which once had belonged to Eetion, Andromache's father, the king of Thebe under Placos, whom Achilles slew.

Last of all, the goddess brought out the glorious arms of Achilles himself, and laid them in the midst, to be the prize of the hero who had saved Achilles's body, and was the bravest and best of the Greeks. Great

Ajax and Odysseus each rose and claimed
them for .himself. Then Nestor said to
Agamemnon, "We other chiefs cannot well
give away this prize ; for to whichever of
these two we give it, the other will be wroth
with us, and will quit our host in his anger.
Let each hero first tell us wherefore he lays
claim to it, and then let the Trojan captives
tell us which they deem has wrought most
harm to Troy."

These terms were agreed upon ; the chiefs
sat in a half-circle ; the people beyond them
pressed eagerly forward to listen, and first
great Ajax rose to speak. Pointing haughtily
to where the fleet lay hauled up on the shore,
he exclaimed—

"Is it in sight of the ships which I saved,
that I am to plead my cause, and that
Odysseus dares to match himself with me?
He soon gave way when Hector came to
burn our ships, what time I met him and
drove him away. In sooth, I need scarcely
tell you of my great deeds, for you have all
beheld them : rather let Odysseus relate what

he has wrought in the dark, when no witness
was near. These arms in any case belong to
me, for Peleus is my uncle, and my father
Telamon sailed with him on board of the
ship Argo, to bring home the golden fleece.
Or shall Odysseus be preferred to me because
he skulked at home, and would fain have
avoided the war by feigning to be mad?
Would that he had been so in truth, or that
his deceit had been believed! We should
not then have to blush for shame when we
think of poor Philoctetes, whom Odysseus
persuaded us to leave at Lemnos. And now
he, our brother-in-arms, bound by the same
oath as ourselves, alone and in misery, limps
about that desert isle, shooting birds with the
arrows of Heracles, which might decide the
fate of Troy, and invoking on the head of
Odysseus the curses that he deserves. Yet
he still lives, because he did not accompany
Odysseus. Unhappy Palamedes had better
have been left behind also: for Odysseus,
ever mindful of how Palamedes found out
his pretence of madness, charged him with

treason, and betrayed an innocent man to death. Thus fights Odysseus, thus is he to be feared. He deserted Nestor in his utmost need, when hampered by his wounded horse, what time Diomedes saved him and bore him away in his own, chariot ; and Diomedes can vouch for the truth of my words. I remember, too, when Odysseus called for aid, and I came to his rescue. He pretended that he was wounded, but when my great shield sheltered him from the foe, he ran off fast enough. On that day, when Hector charged so fiercely, not Odysseus alone, but even brave men turned and fled. I alone withstood him and drove him back. When Hector challenged us all, I accepted his challenge, and was not worsted in the fight. When all the Trojans stormed into our camp to fire the ships, where then was the smooth-tongued Odysseus? Remember that, had the ships been burned, you would never have seen Hellas more: I alone saved them, and for saving so many surely I deserve this reward. Will he compare with these feats of arms his

murder of Dolon in the dark, or his slaughter
of the sleeping Thracians? The credit even
of that exploit belongs more to Diomedes
than to Odysseus; and if you give the arms
to him, you should divide them, and give
Diomedes the larger part. Yet why give
any part at all to this Ithacan, who fights
ever in the dark, by stealth, and unarmed?
The gleam of that golden helmet will but
betray his hiding-place, and warn the foe of
his ambushes. Nor has he strength to wield
the mighty spear of Achilles. Besides, your
shield, Odysseus, which you so seldom expose
to the foe, is as good as new; mine, rent and
torn as it is in a hundred places, is worn
out, and I want a new one. But wherefore
do we dispute in words? let deeds decide
between us. Throw the arms into the midst
of the Trojan host, and whoso brings them back
from thence, let him wear them for his own."

The Greeks loudly cheered brave Ajax
as he sat down, until Odysseus quietly rose
to speak.

"Would to Heaven, princes of Hellas, that

we were not engaged in this dispute, and
Achilles were still with us, able to wear his
own arms.   But since this was not to be,
I think my claim to them is a good one,
because it was I who brought Achilles
hither.   Only, I pray you, do not think
Ajax the better man because he is dull-
witted; nor think the worse of me because
I am a little readier of speech; for these
powers of mine, such as they are, have often
been employed on your behalf, before I
was forced to-day to use them on my own.
As for birth, I am as well born as Ajax, and
my father is not, like his, an exile, guilty of
his brother's blood.   But let us not think of
this, nor let it be counted as a merit to Ajax
that Peleus and Telamon were brothers, but
let us be judged by our own deserts.   Or, if
the next of kin be all that you seek, send the
arms to Peleus in Phthia, or to young Pyrrhus,
whom Deidameia bore to Achilles at Scyros.
What has Ajax to do with them?   Or, if he
claims them, is not Teucer the cousin of
Achilles as well as Ajax?   Yet Teucer, I

trow, does not presume to think that they ought to be his. So, then, since we have but to recount what we ourselves have done, I have more to tell you than I can easily recall to my mind: howbeit, I will start from the beginning and tell all in order. Thetis hid her son at Scyros to save him from the war. No other Greek but I, Ajax least of all, could see through his disguise. I laid spear and shield in his way, and when he seized them and betrayed himself, I bore him off with me to Troy. From henceforth the glory of his deeds belongs to me: it was I who sacked Thebe and Lyrnessus, I who slew fierce Hector. Again, when all the fleet lay wind-bound at Aulis, I won Agamemnon's tardy consent to the sacrifice of his daughter, hard though he pleaded for her life. I, too, went to her mother, and artfully beguiled her into sending the maiden to our camp. Had Ajax gone thither, the Greeks would be at Aulis at this day. Lastly, I was sent to Troy to ask the Trojans to give up Helen. My eloquence prevailed : I won over Priam and Antenor,

and had it not been for Paris and his wild
young brothers, who threatened my life, I
should have succeeded. Menelaus, who went
thither with me, can bear witness to the
truth of what I say. It would take long to
tell all that I have done during our siege.
After the first battle, the Trojans kept
close within their walls. What then did
Ajax do? of what use was he? As for me,
I built the rampart round the ships, I kept
up the spirit of the people, I showed how
they might be fed, I was useful in a hundred
ways. When Agamemnon, deceived by a
dream, bade us launch the ships, Ajax himself made ready to flee, while I held back
the Greeks and reproached them with their
cowardice. Not even in the assembly could
Ajax open his mouth, though the vile Thersites scoffed at Agamemnon, and I soundly
thrashed him for his insolence. Was it a
small feat for me to go forth into the darkness, with only Diomedes for my comrade, to
learn the plans of the foe, and to drive back
in triumph in the car of Rhesus, whom we

slew in the midst of his men? As for Ajax's
boast of having saved the ships, it was
Patroclus who saved them by his charge at
the head of the Myrmidons. As for his duel
with Hector, what was its end? Hector left
the ground unhurt. Ajax forgets, too, that
eight other chiefs, among them myself, were
eager to fight Hector, and that it was only
by lot that he was chosen. When he blames
me for wishing to stay at home, does he not
see that he blames Achilles too? A loving
mother kept back Achilles: I was kept back
by a loving wife. If there was any shame in
this, we both did the same thing, and I am
quite willing to be blamed for doing what
Achilles did. Yet I brought Achilles to our
camp, and saw through his disguise : it was
more than Ajax could do to see through
mine. When Achilles fell I bore his body
on my shoulders, arms and all, though now
Ajax affects to think me too weak to bear
the arms alone. As for Palamedes, all the
host is guilty of his death, not I alone. As
for Philoctetes being left in Lemnos, do not

blame me: all of you agreed to leave him
there, and I will not deny that I advised him
to stay there awhile, and try to heal his bitter
pains by rest. Now that we need his aid, do
not send me : let Ajax rather go to Lemnos,
and try whether by his eloquence he can persuade the angry suffering savage Philoctetes
to rejoin us. Yet, fierce though he be, I
will bring him hither, arrows and all. Do
not whisper to one another, and point to
Diomedes; he is a brave man, and my trusty
comrade. He himself would claim these
arms, did he not know that his hand is more
powerful than his head, and that I surpass
him as much as the pilot of a ship surpasses
him who labours at the oar. You, Ajax,
have strength without reason: I can take
thought for the morrow. You can do
nought but fight: Agamemnon takes counsel
with me as to when it were best for us to
join battle. You are useful only with your
body; I with my mind. Princes of Hellas,
I pray you, bear in mind how I have ever
watched over you, how I have dared, and

still will dare, any risks on your behalf, and give me these arms for my reward."

The chiefs were greatly moved by these words of Odysseus. They asked the Trojan prisoners which of the two heroes had done the most evil to Troy, and they straightway replied, " Odysseus."

Upon this, Odysseus was given the arms, and bore them away in triumph to his tent; but Ajax felt the shame of losing them so keenly that he lost his reason, and that same night stabbed himself with the sword which Hector gave him after their fight.

HOW PHILOCTETES SLEW PARIS

O

CHAPTER XI

How Philoctetes slew Paris

SOON after sunrise on the morrow Menelaus called the Greeks together, and
thus began :

"Princes of Hellas, hear what I advise.
I am pained at heart when I see the people
perishing away here in the war. Too many
of those who came hither to fight for me have
fallen, and will nevermore return to their
parents and their home. Would that I myself had died ere I caused all this host to
gather together, and brought such suffering
upon it. But now let us, as many as are yet
alive, set sail for home. Now that Achilles
and Ajax are both dead, we can never make
head against the Trojans, but many of our

bravest must fall, and only for the sake of me and of Helen. Let Helen stay with the worthless Paris : surely she was mad to leave her pleasant home in Sparta for such a man. I care not for her now, and I cannot bear to see the people die. Let us sail back to Hellas, and leave her here, to bring sorrow upon King Priam and the Trojans."

So spoke he, that he might try the spirit of the Greeks ; for in sooth his heart was hot within him, and he longed to rout the Trojans, break through the walls of Troy, and wreak a dreadful vengeance upon Paris ; for of all the passions that stir men's blood, jealousy is the fiercest. When he sat down the brave Diomedes rose, and sharply up-braided him : saying—

"Son of Atreus, talk not thus cowardly, like unto a woman or a child. Never will the brave Greeks turn back, ere they have cast down all the lofty towers of Troy. Should any one offer to do as you counsel, I will surely smite his head from his shoulders, and throw his carcase to the dogs. But

come, let each chief muster his own people
at their ships, and look well to their armour,
and give both man and horse a plenteous
meal. Then let us march forth to battle,
and let the Immortals judge between us and
the Trojans, which shall win the day."

After Diomedes had spoken, Calchas the
prophet rose, "Hearken unto my- words,"
said he, "for the spirit of prophecy is upon
me. I say unto you that verily you shall
win the lofty city, and that right soon.
Only do that which I bid you, send Odysseus
and Diomedes over the sea to bring hither
young Pyrrhus, the son of great Achilles.
He must be with us ere we can win the
walls of Troy."

"Willingly," said Odysseus, "will I go,
and gladly will I take Diomedes as my
companion. It will be hard if we two cannot persuade the brave boy to come with us,
albeit his mother will weep, and strive to
keep him by her side."

"Odysseus," said Menelaus, "thou prop
and mainstay of the Greeks, if young Pyrrhus

will indeed come hither, and if the Immortals grant him the victory over Troy, I will give him Hermione, my own daughter, for his bride; and I think that he need not be ashamed either of her for his wife, or of me for his father-in-law."

With these words of Menelaus the assembly broke up. Odysseus and Diomedes forthwith launched a swift ship, stored her with food and water, placed twenty stout rowers on board, and set out across the Ægean Sea, to the far off isle of Scyros.

While they were away a great battle was fought. Paris had prevailed upon Telephus, the king of Teuthrania, to send his son Eurypylus to Troy, and he was strong and brave, and pressed the Greeks hard. He slew Peneleus the Boeotian chief, and Machaon the good physician, for whom all alike sorrowed. This at least is true which Pausanias tells, that in the great temple of Asclepius at Pergamus he heard hymns sung in honour of Telephus, who once had been king of the land, but nothing was said in

them about Eurypylus, nor was it permitted
even to mention his name in the temple, for
that men knew him to be the slayer of
Machaon, who was the son of Asclepius.
Teucer the archer gallantly rallied the Greeks,
and saved Machaon's body ; yet when Æneas
and Deiphobus came up, the Greeks gave
way, and were driven quite into their camp.

Meanwhile Odysseus and Diomedes brought
their ship to land at Scyros, where they
found young Pyrrhus practising horsemanship
and hurling the spear. They both were
astonished at his likeness to his father ; and
he straightway addressed them with courteous
words :

" Welcome, strangers, to my house. Tell
me, what are your names, and wherefore have
you journeyed hither across the seas ? "

Odysseus answered :

" We are comrades of great Achilles, who
was, as we are told, your father by the fair
Deidameia ; and indeed you are strangely like
him : but now the Immortals have taken him
to themselves. I come from Ithaca, and my

companion's home is in fertile Argos. I
know not whether you have heard the name
of Diomedes the son of Tydeus, or that of
Odysseus, who now stands before you, sent
by a prophet to bring you to Troy. Take
pity upon us, and come to the camp of the
Greeks, for thus alone can the war be brought
to an end. I myself will bestow upon you
the glorious arms of your father, which will
delight you. They are not like the arms of
mortal men, but such as Ares himself wears
when he goeth forth to battle, so cunningly
hath Hephaestus wrought them as a gift for
your noble father, whom I loved and hon-
oured while he lived, and whose body I
helped to save when he fell. For so doing
Thetis gave me these arms, which I promise
to give you, if you will come with us to Troy.
Moreover, when we shall have taken Troy,
and returned again to our homes, Menelaus
will give you his bright-haired daughter
Hermione for your bride, and many rich
gifts with her : for he is a wealthy king."

Then answered the brave son of Achilles :

"If of a truth the Fates bid me go to Troy,
I will go thither with you on the morrow
across the sea, and will do what I can to help
the Greeks. But now you are my guests,
and must feast with me to-night. As for
my marriage, we will think of that hereafter."

So saying, he led them into the palace,
where they found the fair Deidameia, wasting away with grief for her lost Achilles,
even as snow upon the mountains wastes
away in the heat of the summer sun. Pyrrhus told her the names of his guests, but did
not tell her the errand on which they were
come. She feasted them royally, and they
slept that night in her palace; but Deidameia
lay awake the whole night long, listening to
the moan of the surf against the rocky shore
of Scyros, and foreboding evil from the coming of Odysseus. He had come to Scyros
once before, what time he took her darling
Achilles from her, and bore him away to the
war, where he died. Since that day neither
she nor old Peleus had ever ceased to grieve,
and now she feared Odysseus was come to

take away her boy also. In the morning she clung to Pyrrhus, weeping bitterly, and said, "Child, surely you are not going away with these our guests to that hateful Troy, where already so many of the bravest have met their death? You are too young, and have not skill to meet fierce warriors in battle. Hearken to my words: abide with me here at home, and let me not hear the tidings of your death at Troy: for I cannot hope ever to see you return. Even your father perished there, albeit he was stronger by far than you, and though a goddess was his mother. Therefore I tremble when I think that I shall be robbed of you too, my child; for women know no keener grief than when their husbands and their children die, leaving them desolate widows in a house of mourning, wronged by their neighbours, and with none to help them."

So spoke she, piteously wailing: but Pyrrhus answered her:

"Cheer up, mother, and be not over-anxious. I shall not fall unless it be my fate, which no man can avoid : but if I must die, I hope that it will not come to pass ere I have done some brave deed of arms, worthy of the race from which I come."

Old King Lycomedes now entered the chamber, and wished Pyrrhus a prosperous voyage, warning him of the dangers of the seas; and Pyrrhus, though eager to start, yet stayed a while to comfort his mother, who could not bear to be parted from him. After many embraces he at last tore himself away, and Deidameia, through all her tears, felt proud of her son.

While the ship sped merrily eastward, Pyrrhus asked Odysseus many questions about the war, and about who were the bravest chiefs on either side, until they drew near to the lonely isle of Lemnos.

" We must land here," said Odysseus, " for I must see Philoctetes, and try to prevail upon him to come with us to Troy. At any rate I must get his bow and arrows, for without them Troy can never be taken."

Saying thus, Odysseus steered the ship to

the beach, and he and Pyrrhus landed, leaving Diomedes with the ship. While they
were doing thus, Philoctetes was watching
them from his cave on the mountain side.
His hair was shaggy and matted, and his
eyes were sunken and wild-looking. He
was lean, and brown, and wasted; for he had
been long alone on the island, and the wound
in his foot had never healed. When first he
saw them coming up the path which led to
his cave, he seized his bow and fitted an
arrow to the string : but when he recognised
Odysseus, he felt a wish to speak to his old
comrade once more, in spite of the hatred he
bore him for having left him there. He
wished also to learn the name of the tall
youth by Odysseus's side, who reminded him
of a well-known figure : and, musing thus,
he laid aside his weapons, and awaited the
approach of the strangers.

When Odysseus came to the cave, he
greeted Philoctetes, told him who Pyrrhus
was, and begged him to come with them to
Troy. Philoctetes, in spite of his dislike to

Odysseus, answered him courteously, but declared that he was unable to leave the island, by reason of the agony caused him by his wounded foot. He was no longer able to take part in a battle, and shrank from meeting his fellow-men. The birds which he shot supplied him with food, and their skins served him for clothing. He flatly refused to leave his cave; and at length Odysseus left off pressing him to undertake the journey ; but, while Philoctetes limped away with young Pyrrhus to show him a fountain at which he was wont to drink, Odysseus seized the famous bow and arrows of Heracles, and quickly made his way to the ship with them. When Pyrrhus joined him there, Odysseus showed him the weapons in triumph, and was for setting sail forthwith: but Pyrrhus's generous heart had been touched by the sight of poor Philoctetes in his cave, suffering and alone. He declared that he never would be guilty of so treacherous a deed, took the bow and arrows away from Odysseus, and carried them back to Philoctetes.

When Philoctetes returned to his cave and found that Odysseus had stolen his beloved bow and arrows, he sank down upon the earth and gave himself up for lost. He could no longer hope to provide himself with food, for he never could make another bow, crippled and helpless as he was. While he was bitterly lamenting his cruel fate, and the base treachery with which he had been treated, he saw Pyrrhus again coming towards him, and no words can tell with what joy he received his darling weapons from the noble-hearted young hero. In his delight he forgot both the pain of his wound and his anger against Odysseus, and declared that he would follow Pyrrhus to Troy, and never leave him again, for he had saved his life, and had taught him that kindness was still to be found among men.

When they came to Troy, they found the Greeks unable to stir from their camp, and mourning for Machaon, Peneleus, and the other chiefs who had been slain. Podalirius, with the help and blessing of the Immortals,

soon cured the wound in Philoctetes's foot,
and ere many days had passed both he and
Pyrrhus made ready for battle. The Greeks
were overjoyed when they beheld Pyrrhus
wearing the well-known armour of Achilles,
and almost believed that they had got his
father back again, so like was he to Achilles
in face and form.

Nor were they disappointed when Pyrrhus
led forth his Myrmidons to battle, for he lightly
wielded the great spear of his father, which
old Cheiron had cut from an ash-tree on
Mount Pelion, and with it he struck down
man after man, until at last he fought and
slew the terrible Eurypylus himself. Philoctetes, also, bore himself bravely. No longer
a squalid savage, but looking like the hero
that he was, glittering with the splendid
arms of Heracles, he proudly led his men
once more, and fought ever in the front
rank. Round his waist was a golden belt,
embossed with figures of wild beasts ; and
across his shoulders was slung his bow-case,
of marvellous workmanship. On it was

figured Hermes slaying Argus of the hundred eyes, and Phaethon falling from the chariot of the Sun, while the earth beneath him looked scorched and blackened, so well was it wrought. There, too, was Perseus with the terrible head of Medusa, the stream of Ocean, and the baths of all the stars, and there was Prometheus lying upon the peak of Caucasus, in chains of adamant, while the eagle plucked at his heart. Such noble gifts had Hephaestus wrought for the mighty Heracles.

When the day was far spent, Paris met Philoctetes. Little did Paris dream that his last day had dawned, as he marked his comrade Polydamas strike Cleodorus, the Rhodian, a terrible blow with his battle-axe, which cut the strap by which his shield was slung upon his shoulder. As Cleodorus drew back, still holding his spear, but no longer covered by his shield, Paris aimed at Philoctetes, but missed him, and pierced the breast of Cleodorus with a mortal wound.

At this Philoctetes took a steady aim at Paris, shouting as he did so:

"Dog, you shall surely die, now that you have dared to match yourself with me : and glad will all men be when they see you fall."

He drew the string, bent his bow into a circle, and let fly his arrow.   It only grazed Paris on the hand ; but as Paris was making ready to shoot in his turn, Philoctetes sent a second arrow deep into his flank.

Paris shrieked with the pain of his wound, and rushed away to the rear, where the physicians bound it up.   When it grew dark, the fighting came to an end, and Greeks and Trojans each sought their homes ; but Paris never went back to his home in Troy.   Faint and dizzy he staggered along, all alone, through the dark thickets of Mount Ida which he knew so well.   Foul birds of night flitted around him with ominous cries, and the pain of his wound warned him that death was near.   Yet he walked on until he came to where his deserted wife, Œnone, dwelt, but when he came into her presence he sank at her feet like one already dead.

Then, while she looked on astonished, he revived a little, and faintly said to her:

"Mine own true wife : forgive me that I left you. Would that I had died in your arms ere Aphrodite beguiled me away from you to seek for Helen. Now I implore you, by the Immortals who dwell above us, and by the memory of our wedded love, show me some kindness, and heal me this grievous wound, which fills my veins with fire, and drains away my life. You can save me if you will; for you well know all the virtues of precious-juiced flowers, and the drugs that take away disease. Pity me, and let me not die thus at your feet, lest the Gods be angry, and send the Furies to punish you for your hardness of heart; for prayers are the daughters of Immortal Zeus. Forgive me for the wrong which I have done to you, and show mercy on me now."

So he spoke : but she harshly answered him :

"Wherefore have you come hither to me? to me whom you left to weep here alone, while you took your pleasure with the fair daughter of Tyndareus. Go back to her, if she is so much better than your own true wife. Ask her to heal your wounds, and do not come bewailing them to me. Would that I had the strength of a wild beast, to rend you to pieces: so might I wreak a fitting vengeance for the sorrow you have brought upon me. Go, hateful alike to gods and to men. Where now is Aphrodite, in whom you put your trust? Let her be your helper. Go, seek your Helen, and leave me alone with my sorrows."

So spoke Œnone, her once gentle heart swelling with jealous rage, and Paris wandered wearily away into the night. As soon as he was gone, Œnone would fain have called him back, for she felt in her heart that she loved him still: and all night long she lay grieving for him, and repenting her that she had not helped him in his agony.

On the morrow a shepherd came to Hecuba, and told her that he had found the dead body of Paris lying on Mount Ida. His father and mother wept over him, and

Helen was sore distressed, not so much for Paris as for herself; for she dared not flee away to the camp of the Greeks, and yet she feared to remain in Troy, because of the anger of the people against her.

When Œnone heard of the dreadful end of Paris, she shrieked aloud, crying:

"Woe is me, for my wickedness and folly. Life is hateful to me now. Once in happier days I hoped that I and Paris might grow old together, and that our love would never fade away. Would that I had died when Paris deserted me. But though he left me when alive, I will rejoin him now that he is dead. I will dare to die, for I can no longer bear to live."

So saying, she rushed wildly away to where the shepherds of Mount Ida were burning the body of Paris upon a funeral pile. There she covered her face with her mantle, leaped into the midst of the flames, and perished with him, faithful to the last. All the nymphs her sisters wept for her, and said:

"Of a truth Paris cannot have been in his

right mind, not to care for so noble a wife
as Œnone, who loved him more than she
loved her own life, even though he deserted
her for another."

That day, as Odysseus was scouting about,
far away from the camp, as was his wont, he
espied a solitary figure straying near the skirts
of Mount Ida. He straightway gave chase,
and soon came up with the stranger, who
proved to be the son of Priam, the Trojan
seer Helenus. Odysseus brought him prisoner
to the camp, and there learned from him
that, when the death of Paris became known
in Troy, Helenus and Deiphobus had fought
for Helen. Deiphobus had worsted Helenus,
who in his anger had left the city, and given
himself up, nothing loth, to Odysseus. Moreover, Helenus told Odysseus that an ancient
prophecy declared that Troy never could be
taken, as long as the holy image of Pallas
remained in her temple in the citadel.

HOW THE GREEKS TOOK TROY

CHAPTER XII

How the Greeks took Troy

WHEN evening was come, Odysseus, who had told no one what he had learned from Helenus, made up his mind to essay to carry off the image of Pallas, albeit it was kept in the temple of the goddess, in Pergamus, the innermost citadel of Troy. He disguised himself as a beggar, hid a sharp sword under his rags, and, accompanied by Diomedes alone, set off towards Troy. When they were come to the city, Diomedes stayed behind in a hiding-place near the walls, while Odysseus, who had disfigured himself with dirt and scratches, went up to the gate and began to beg for alms. The guard took no heed of him, and allowed him to pass into the city. He had been there once before, and this now stood him in good stead, for he was able to find his way through the streets up to the citadel.

He asked alms of all whom he met, the better to support his disguise, and no one recognised him till, just without the gate of the temple of Pallas, he suddenly came upon Helen, who had been praying to the goddess, and was now returning to her home. Helen saw in a moment who he was, and what danger he was in. She hurriedly drew him into her house, shut and barred the door, and said:

" Odysseus, what new plot is this? How dared you enter Troy alone? surely yours is an iron heart. But tell me, what are the plans of the Greeks, and what hope have they of winning the city? Will my husband Menelaus take me back, or will he stab me to the heart when he meets me? If so, it were better for me to die here in Troy."

So spoke Helen, weeping, and Odysseus made reply:

" The Greeks can never win the city,

while yonder holy image of Pallas remains
in her temple.   They say that it fell from
heaven, and was not wrought by the hands
of mortal men.   So now I have come to take
it away, and this night the deed must be
done.   My comrade Diomedes waits without,
and we two together can easily overpower the
guard of the temple, and steal the holy image,
if only you, fair lady, help us ; and I know
that you will."

While bold Odysseus spoke thus, Helen
smiled upon him, admiring his courage and
his ready wit.   Odysseus thought that he
had never seen her look more lovely, for her
beauty remained as of yore, unharmed by time
and sorrow.   Then she said :

" O would that I had never come hither,
leaving my pleasant home in Sparta !   Surely
I was mad when I hearkened to Paris : would
that I had died first.   And now, if the Greeks
take Troy, who can tell what fate awaits me ?
Yet you are a Greek, and I cannot but help
you, for my heart yearns after my countrymen.
Come with me : I will show you how you

must make the attempt. It is now night, and the darkness will hide you from your foes."

So saying, Helen guided Odysseus through the city to a postern gate, by which she let in Diomedes. She then led them up to the temple, bade them carefully mark the way by which they had come, and returned to her own house. Odysseus and Diomedes forced their way into the temple, and while Odysseus stabbed the guardian, Alcathous, to the heart, lest he should give the alarm, Diomedes seized the holy image, gave his spear to Odysseus to carry, and retreated as fast as he could. As they passed through the deserted streets, the moon suddenly shone out from behind a cloud. Diomedes, who walked first, started, as he saw behind his own shadow on the wall the shadow of a figure about to thrust at him with a spear. He straightway turned round, and found himself face to face with Odysseus. Then the thought struck him that Odysseus was jealous of his share in the adventure, and would fain have slain him, and gained all the glory for himself. Whether Diomedes was right or not, I cannot tell; but he made Odysseus walk in front of him all the rest of the way back to the camp.

After the Palladium had been carried off, the Greeks felt sure that Troy must fall. Yet when they would have stormed the walls, the Trojans beat them back : and at last Calchas warned them that they must win the city by art, and not by force.   When all were at their wits' end to know how this might be, Odysseus devised a cunning stratagem.

"Let us," said he, "build a great wooden horse, and place within it all our bravest heroes.   Then let the rest burn their tents, launch their ships, and set sail as though they meant to return home: but let them leave one man behind, with his hands tied behind his back, besmeared with dirt and blood : and let him be some one whose face is not known to the Trojans.   When the ships go away, the Trojans will pour forth from their city to look at the Greek camp, and will find the wooden horse standing there. Then this man will come forward, and tell them that the Greeks made the horse as an offering to Pallas Athênê, to turn away her wrath for the theft of her holy image. He will also tell them that he himself is a stranger, and that the Greeks intended to sacrifice him to the gods, to obtain a fair wind, even as they sacrificed Iphigenia before leaving Aulis, but that he escaped from them just in time, and wandered about in the plight in which they see him. If he tells his story well, the Trojans will be sure to take the wooden horse into their citadel, to replace the holy image which they have lost; and we will build it so large that it cannot pass through the gates, but that a breach must be made in the walls to get it through. When they have taken it into their city and placed it in the citadel, I am sure they will keep a careless watch. Then our spy must raise a great fire beacon upon the topmost tower, as a signal to the fleet, which will be at Tenedos, and he must go to the horse, and let out the heroes who are hid within it. The rest of the Greeks will re-land, make their way through the breach in the walls, and Troy will be ours."

When Odysseus proposed this plan, most of the Greeks thought well of it, and were eager to carry it out; but young Pyrrhus and Philoctetes disliked it, and said that Troy could only be won by sheer hard fighting. Nevertheless Calchas won their consent, and now all called upon Epeus, the son of Panopeus, to build the horse, because he was the cleverest workman in all the host, and had been taught his craft by Athênê herself. Men say that Athênê visited Epeus that night in a dream, and showed him how he must begin to build. Agamemnon sent forth the people to cut down trees on Mount Ida, and all worked hard, under the orders of Epeus, until he had fashioned a noble horse, and carved its head and mane and flowing tail so that it looked as though it were alive. When the horse was finished, all men wondered at it : but Odysseus said:

" Princes of Hellas, the time has come to prove which of you are the stoutest of heart,

for now a desperate deed must be done. We
must hide ourselves within the horse, and
take what fortune may befall us; for either
we shall win Troy, after all our fruitless years
of toil, or we shall be found out and die. As
soon as we are all inside, the rest of you
must burn the tents, launch the ships, sail to
Tenedos, and wait there watching till you
see the beacon blaze from Troy. And let
some brave youth, whose face the Trojans
have not seen, be left behind, and tell them
the tale that we have planned."

Then one Sinon, a grandson of the crafty
Autolycus, who was but lately come to the
war, stood forth, and said that he dared to be
that man. All the host wondered at him,
for never before had he shown such courage.
While they were binding his hands and making him ready to play his part, Nestor en-
couraged the heroes who were going up into
the hollow belly of the horse, telling them
that the sight put him in mind of the day
when Jason bade his gallant crew take their
places on board of the ship Argo, what time

he set sail from Iolcos by the sea, to bring
back the golden fleece. Nestor went with
them then, though Pelias would fain have
kept him at home: and now, old as he was,
he wished to go into the horse with the other
heroes, and to share their glory : but young
Pyrrhus courteously bade him rather go to
Tenedos with the fleet, and watch for the
signal for return. Nestor tenderly embraced
Pyrrhus, for he loved him dearly, both for
his father's sake and for his own, and then
the chosen heroes went up the ladder into the
hollow horse. First went Pyrrhus the son of
Achilles, and next to him bold Menelaus.
Then came Odysseus, Sthenelus, and Diomedes. Next were Philoctetes, Menestheus;
Thoas, and Polypoetes: and then came Ajax,
the son of Oileus, Eurypylus of Hypereia,
Nestor's son Thrasymedes, Idomeneus with
his friend Meriones, and Podalirius the
physician, Teucer the archer, Leontes, Demo-
phoon and Acamas, the sons of Theseus, and
many another hero besides, until there was
no room for more. Last of all came Epeus,

the maker of the horse, because he knew best how to fasten up the door by which they came in.

As soon as all these heroes were fast shut up within the great wooden horse, the others burned their camp, launched their ships, and sailed away towards the West.

There was brave feasting in the fair city of Troy that night. Spears and shields were hung high upon the walls, and in every street was heard music and dancing, the shouts of banqueters and the voice of minstrelsy. Fast went the wine-cup round from hand to hand, and merrily the Trojans pledged one another in high carousal, now that their long siege was at an end at last, and their own eyes had seen the hated Greeks sail away. In careless jollity they revelled on, long after the sun had set, until the moon shone out, pouring her soft light for the last time upon the fair city, as it stood with all its palaces and temples clearly outlined, and all the mighty circuit of its walls distinctly shown,

all unbroken save only where the fatal horse
had been dragged through. Sinon had told
his story well. The walls had been breached.
The horse with its fateful freight had been
placed before the temple of Pallas in the
citadel; and now, as all the Trojans were
sinking into a heavy dreamless sleep, Sinon,
who had shared their feast, stole gently
through the silent streets towards the high
watch-tower. No guard was there : no
watch was kept : all slept or revelled still.
Trembling lest he should be seen, Sinon fired
the beacon, and while the sky blushed ruddy
with its blaze, he made his way to the citadel,
to where the great wooden horse gleamed
white in the moonbeams. Here he called
in a low voice to the heroes within, not
daring to speak aloud, lest some Trojan
might overhear him. The heroes, who had
anxiously watched for this signal, asked
Odysseus in whispers whether the time was
come for them to sally forth from their
narrow prison; but he would not suffer them
to leave the horse, eager though they were,

before he himself had carefully peered out through the openings on either side, even as a famished wolf who means to fall upon a sheepfold, and who first looks round with earnest care to see whether men or dogs are near to protect it. Even so did Odysseus look all around, and then the chiefs came forth, down the ladder which Epeus had contrived for them. Each man's heart beat loud as he grasped his weapons and made ready to fall upon the sleeping city. Then they dashed in the doors of the nearest houses, and began to burn and slay : the rest of the host poured in through the breach in the walls, and Troy was won.

Odysseus and Menelaus, who knew their way through the streets, went straightway to the house of Deiphobus, where Helen dwelt now that Paris was dead. As they passed the house of Antenor, they hung up a panther's skin over his door, a signal agreed upon with the rest of the Greeks that they should spare it, for they wished to save the good old man, who had shown them kindness when they

came to Troy before. When they broke
into the house of Deiphobus, he was asleep,
but at the noise of their entrance he started
up and seized his weapons, while Helen fled
screaming as she saw Menelaus, and knew
that Troy was won. Deiphobus, albeit taken
by surprise and without armour, fought
bravely, but ere long Menelaus overpowered
him, struck him dead, and fiercely hacked
and mauled his body in the frenzy of his
rage. With the bloody sword still in his
hand he then turned towards Helen. For a
while he gazed upon her, as she stood in the
bright light of the blazing city; for he meant
to slay her also : but as he looked upon her
surpassing beauty he forgot his purpose, and
all the wrong which she had done him. He
let his sword fall to the ground, took her
gently by the hand, and led her away in
silence.

Meanwhile Pyrrhus had burst open the
doors of Priam's royal palace, and forced his
way into the great court within. Here, hard
by the altar of Zeus, stood old Priam, who

had hastily snatched up a spear and shield. When Pyrrhus came before him, gleaming in the splendid armour of Achilles, bright as a snake that has newly cast its skin, the old king struck feebly at him with his spear, but Pyrrhus struck him dead, and rushed forward to see if any of the Trojans still resisted.

When the first alarm was given, Æneas had called together a few brave men, and strove hard to drive back the Greeks; but ere long all his comrades were either slain or forced away from his side. As a gallant sailor stands at the helm of a ship in a tempest, and steers her skilfully until he feels that she is ready to sink beneath his feet, and then gets into a little boat to save his own life, and rows away, caring no longer for the great ship, even so Æneas felt that Troy was lost, and that he could do nought to save her. He raised his aged father Anchises upon his broad shoulders, took his little son Ascanius by the hand, and made his way safely out of the burning city, through all the ranks of the triumphant Greeks : for Aphrodite his mother watched over him, and shielded him from harm. And how he sailed away and founded Rome ; and how Menelaus forgave his wife Helen, and lived with her in Sparta to a good old age ; and how Odysseus wandered for years before he could reach his little isle of Ithaca, and his faithful wife Penelope ; and how Agamemnon went home to Mycenae, and was basely slain by Clytemnestra, out of revenge for the death of Iphigenia, has all been written by the ancients themselves, in some of the noblest poetry in the world, which you may read for yourself some day.

THE END.